"**We're not partners, Dex!**" Beth shouted, whacking him with the pillow. "**We're two chiefs with no Indians.**"

"I don't want to boss you around!" He caught her on the backside. "I care about you!"

"You have a funny way of showing it!" She launched herself onto the bed and Dex went down with a grunt. Taking advantage of his vulnerable position, she straddled him and threw his pillow aside. Then she tossed hers away, and pinned his hands over his head. She shook her hair from her face. "Give up."

"No way, lady," he said, bucking underneath her. But she'd wrestled with her cousins and never lost. Dex couldn't beat her. In her triumph, she didn't notice the fire in his gray eyes.

"Say uncle, and I'll let you up!" she insisted.

"Not on your life!"

Suddenly she sensed him moving under her. A blast of numbing heat shot through her. "Admit it," she said, her voice more a purr than a growl.

"Admit what?" he murmured hoarsely. "That I want you? That I won't be able to sleep across from you when your scent fills the room tonight? Admit that the sheen of your hair on the pillow, the glow of your skin makes me want to lean over and caress you?" His fingers merged with hers. "I'll admit that."

"No!" Her mind told her to move, but her traitorous body refused. How could she move when her blood sizzled and her skin burned with his fire? "Give up," she demanded, her lips brushing his.

"No, you give up," he murmured, his breath sweet in her mouth.

"Never!" With a moan she met his lips in a kiss that whirled them both into a hurricane of sensation. . . .

WHAT ARE *LOVESWEPT* ROMANCES?

They are stories of true romance and touching emotion. We believe those two very important ingredients are constants in our highly sensual and very believable stories in the *LOVESWEPT* line. Our goal is to give you, the reader, stories of consistently high quality that may sometimes make you laugh, sometimes make you cry, but are always fresh and creative and contain many delightful surprises within their pages.

Most romance fans read an enormous number of books. Those they truly love, they keep. Others may be traded with friends and soon forgotten. We hope that each *LOVESWEPT* romance will be a treasure—a "keeper." We will always try to publish

LOVE STORIES YOU'LL NEVER FORGET
BY AUTHORS YOU'LL ALWAYS REMEMBER

The Editors

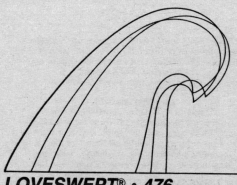

LOVESWEPT® • 476

Courtney Henke
In a Golden Web

BANTAM BOOKS
NEW YORK • TORONTO • LONDON • SYDNEY • AUCKLAND

IN A GOLDEN WEB

A Bantam Book / June 1991

If you would be interested in receiving protective vinyl
covers for your Loveswept books, please write to this address
for information:

Loveswept
Bantam Books
P.O. Box 985
Hicksville, NY 11802

ISBN 0-553-44159-0

Published simultaneously in the United States and Canada

Bantam Books are published by Bantam Books, a division
of Bantam Doubleday Dell Publishing Group, Inc. Its trademark, consisting of the words "Bantam Books" and the
portrayal of a rooster, is Registered in U.S. Patent and
Trademark Office and in other countries. Marca Registrada.
Bantam Books, 666 Fifth Avenue, New York, New York
10103.

PRINTED IN THE UNITED STATES OF AMERICA

OPM   0 9 8 7 6 5 4 3 2 1

Dedication

To Laura, who kept me together when I felt like falling apart; to JacobsDad, who told me everything I ever wanted to know about real names; and of course to Kurt, who finally came home and made my life complete once more.

One

It was like a scene from a movie, Elizabeth Hamner decided as she entered her department at the bank. The clerks who always scurried to their desks when the "Velvet Hammer" descended on the room now peered around their computer screens, keyboards silent. Though San Francisco was full of oddities, a corporate thief obviously outshined even old Joe, the janitor who thought he was Eleanor Roosevelt. He'd never rated more than a passing glance, despite his atrocious taste in gowns.

She tilted her chin up a notch, resisting the impulse to shriek out her innocence. No matter what the current investigation revealed, no matter how much circumstantial evidence the police dredged up in this embezzlement case, as long as she legally retained her authority, she refused to allow her division—or her emotions—to regress to a state of chaos. "Impulsive" was simply not in her vocabulary.

With the self-command her Marine father had drilled into her from birth, she turned her smoothly coiffed blonde head a single degree, raised one carefully etched brow, and gave the ghouls a full dose of her ice-blue eyes. "Do we all need something more to do?" she inquired in the silky, hard-edged voice that had earned her her nickname. If only they knew how off the mark the nickname really was, she thought.

The workers stilled, then paled. Suddenly the room hummed with activity. Elizabeth wondered if some Kansas dirt farmer had acquired a million Swiss francs while they'd gawked. After giving them a last look that she hoped was menacing rather than vulnerable, she spun toward her office.

She halted midstride as slow, rhythmic applause cut through the buzz of the office, each accentuated clap making the sound an affront instead of a tribute. Pivoting, she saw two men step out from the shadow of an artistically placed ficus.

Her heart slammed into her ribs as she recognized one of the men immediately. The grizzled, squat, and wickedly intelligent Lieutenant Harry Shaw was unmistakable, reminding her of a stock character in an old gangster film. But he hadn't been the one who'd given her the taunting accolade.

No, it had been the act of the second man. As she turned toward him, thunder rumbled outside, a fitting, dramatic sound effect for this moment. The man with the familiar rugged features and mocking smile faced her, watching her from beneath round, wire-rim glasses. Giving a final clap, he lowered his hands. It took all her self-discipline not to fling herself at him with bared teeth.

She wanted to excuse her irrational urge as a normal reaction to the booming thunder, but, if the truth be told, it was a reaction to the man himself. She'd initially met Dexter Wolffe two years before, after he'd installed the original security program in the bank's computer system. Armed with nothing but a high school degree and an overblown idea of his own importance, he'd slithered to the top of his profession, then tossed it all away a decade ago to free-lance.

They had become adversaries at first sight.

And now that the tawny-haired egotist had compiled the so-called evidence against her—beginning the collapse of her banking career—she couldn't stand to be in the same room with him. She kept telling herself it had nothing to do with the way he looked at her—as if he knew her innermost secrets.

"Lieutenant." She acknowledged the plain-clothesman with a regal nod, deciding to blatantly ignore Wolffe as she would a whining mosquito. "Do you have more questions for me? Or does your bird dog already have all the answers, as usual?"

She regretted her last comment instantly. By admitting the man existed she had ruined both insults, and his answering chuckle only confirmed her suspicions.

"Aren't we touchy this afternoon," Wolffe marveled as he pushed the sleeves of his cable-knit sweater to his elbows. "Did the prime rate drop again, Ms. Hamner? Or has intimidating your latest secretary lost its thrill?"

She had to tilt her chin up to meet his gaze. To

her dismay, her only concrete thoughts revolved around his awesome height, and a lament that hackers were supposed to look like Pee Wee Herman, not Harrison Ford. Luckily, her competitive nature took over.

"Why, Mr. Wolffe, finished so soon?" Her mouth rounded in an O of surprise. "Of course, how silly of me! You must have another persecution scheduled for after lunch."

The muscle in his square jaw quivered. "My schedule's flexible, Ms. Hamner. Unlike people, machines patiently wait for their information instead of jumping to conclusions."

"They jumped pretty fast this time," she muttered. "You should be careful of the company you keep, Lieutenant," she said with a patently false smile, keeping her gaze firmly fixed on her opponent. "People might assume you're an exterminator instead of a police officer." Someday, she warned Dexter silently, she would wipe that smirk off his face—with pleasure. "Or was that your intention?"

Wolffe's gray eyes glittered behind his glasses, indicating his acceptance of her unspoken challenge. "Actually, I'm just here to pick up my fee." He crossed his muscular arms over his chest. "I'm off the case."

His statement surprised her so much, she didn't voice her next biting comment. Her gaze flew to Lieutenant Shaw, who calmly popped a piece of peppermint gum into his mouth. "What's going on?" she asked, hope struggling to life inside of her. "Did you find Jane? Have you made an arrest?"

Shaw shook his head. "Your ex-assistant picked

a lousy time to go on vacation." His tone was suspicious.

Elizabeth was quick to justify Jane's absence. "Even before she moved to Arizona, Jane always left this time of year, to celebrate her twin daughters' birthday."

"Well, she's due back this evening, but I'm afraid it's not my problem now. As of ten minutes ago, the federal authorities are in charge." Shaw's disdain was obvious.

A wave of icy fear swept over her. The lieutenant was the only one who believed in her. And federal involvement meant publicity, which meant pressure from shareholders, outraged cries for a quick arrest, public humiliation. This new development meant it was no longer an embezzlement case involving a few missing local dollars; it was now a national concern. She would be arrested before nightfall.

"Are the Feds going after Jane?" she asked, appalled at the quaver in her voice.

Shaw hesitated. "I don't think so."

"But she's the key to my innocence," she whispered, then started as she felt the warmth of a touch on her shoulder. She saw a tanned, sinewy hand resting there. Her eyes focused on the odd ring Dexter Wolffe always wore, a black opal etched with the figure of a spider, and for some idiotic reason she felt safe.

Determined to live up to her nickname, she plucked the offending member from her shoulder and brushed off the burgundy linen. "I would hate to catch anything," she told him acidly.

He dropped his arm to his side, his mocking smile firmly back in place. "I don't think you need to worry. Any self-respecting germ would be scared off by the competition."

"You should know," she said, then turned away and strode to her office before he could comment.

Unobtrusively, she wiped a clammy palm down her burgundy suit skirt. At her pocket, paper crackled, reminding her of the note she'd received. Another damned threatening note.

She opened her mouth to call to the policeman as he stood at the elevator, then closed it with a snap. It wasn't his problem, he'd told her. As usual, it was no one's problem but hers.

For an instant, the urge to bolt was so strong that she could taste the fresh air on her tongue. Damn, she thought. Her tightly reined panic was bubbling too near the surface. And if she let it loose, if she dropped her guard for a single moment, the world would know that the Hammer's rigid facade concealed a mere mortal. She couldn't afford that—not now, not ever.

At the thought, she met Dexter's intense gray eyes across the room. Though she automatically pasted a sneer on her lips, she froze in her doorway, a solution flaring to life in her mind with awesome clarity. It was crazy, it was irrational, but she couldn't sit around twiddling her thumbs watching the Feds and the real embezzler rip apart everything she'd worked so hard to achieve! Unlike Dexter Wolffe, she was a doer, not an onlooker.

Obviously, she needed to locate Jane herself.

She blinked, astonished at the simplicity of her plan. All she had to do was slip unseen out of the building, fly to Phoenix, and get back before anyone knew she was gone. It was not an impulse, she told herself quickly. It was strategy in its purest form.

As her gaze remained focused on the man beside the elevator, her mouth widened in a smile that had made weaker men run for cover. Her plan had a certain poetic justice, she decided.

"You got me into this," she murmured to the distant figure. "You'll be my ticket out."

Dex watched Elizabeth as she whirled into her office, wondering at the emotion he thought he'd glimpsed in those ice-blue eyes, a flash that, for an instant, made her seem . . . defenseless.

He shook off the thought, telling himself she was about as vulnerable as a cactus. "She's up to something, Harry," he told his longtime friend. "When that shark in panty hose bares her teeth, it means trouble for the rest of the little fishies."

"I wish you'd stop picking on her," Harry said quietly. "You're confusing her with Amber, Dex, because she's a smart, successful woman. Don't blame her for what Amber did to you. Elizabeth's in a lot of trouble. The Feds think her witness is a stalling tactic."

"Don't you?" Dex asked, frowning.

"I don't know."

Irritated by his own impressions, Dex murmured, "It doesn't matter. She can take care of herself." He wished he didn't feel a stab of admiration. "She's the Velvet Hammer, Harry. Women like her eat corporations for breakfast. The Feds'll never know what hit 'em."

"Maybe." The elevator doors whooshed open, but Harry didn't enter. At Dex's questioning look, he shrugged, snapping his gum. "The Captain says I'm supposed to *cooperate* with the suits." He snorted. "But I've decided it's time for that long-overdue vacation." He glanced toward Elizabeth's office. "I'm getting too old for this crap."

Dex told himself it wasn't his problem, either. So what if the trail leading to Elizabeth was one a child could follow? So what if they hadn't given him enough time to trace the actual cash to its hiding place? His job was finished. "Have fun, Harry. I'm going to cash my check, go home, and sit in the hot tub for about a million years." He attempted a smile, trying to dredge up his old antagonism toward their suspect. "I'd really hoped you cops paid better. I was in the mood for champagne and cavier."

"Hey!" Harry stopped the portals from closing. "Go easy on the celebration, friend. She is innocent, you know."

Dex met Harry's gaze solidly, longing to quell his guilt. "Yeah, I know," he said softly. "I just don't know how I know."

Harry nodded and released the door. "I figured as much."

Elizabeth grabbed her raincoat and clutch purse, transferring the note and a slip of paper with Jane's unlisted phone number into it. Then she strode with her customary ground-eating pace toward the elevator.

During the longest five minutes of her entire life, she peeked around a pylon in the parking garage to watch reporters with Minicams gather beneath dripping umbrellas outside the wire-mesh security gate. Her stomach methodically tied itself in a knot as she wondered if she was doing the right thing. But she shook off the doubt. Jane Ward was her only hope. For a year Elizabeth had fought for Jane's promotion to the regional manager's slot in Phoenix, but the others had vetoed Elizabeth's choice, because they didn't want another woman with too much power in the upper echelons. Then, four months ago, someone had secretly pushed the advancement through. Single-parent Jane had accepted and had moved her family bag and baggage to Phoenix.

According to the police, the systematic drain of funds had begun a month before she'd left. Though Elizabeth didn't believe her protege was in on the conspiracy, she knew Jane *must* have seen something—or someone—she shouldn't have to warrant her getting the promotion out of town.

By the time Dexter Wolffe finally stepped into the garage, Elizabeth was ready to scream with tension. Instead she slipped on her raincoat, shoved one hand inside, gripped her purse in the other, then crept toward her unsuspecting prey.

As she raised her hand under her coat pocket, her "weapon" poking into the material, Dexter whirled and caught her shoulders in his strong hands. Unprepared for his quick reaction, she couldn't avoid her breasts being crushed against his hard chest. He had her pinned like a rabbit in headlights. For such a lazy-looking man, she thought numbly, he had the reflexes of a panther.

"Why, Ms. Hamner," he said calmly. "Is that a gun in your pocket, or are you happy to see me?"

She stared dazedly at his sensual mouth, a

breath away from hers, but his words reminded her of her purpose. "It's—it's a 9-millimeter Beretta pistol," she said, pulling the description out of thin air. It was a wonder her brain worked at all. Gulping, she squelched the odd sensations and drew on her strength of will.

She stepped back, wishing her nipples didn't have a memory of their own. They still tingled like a Geiger counter in the presence of uranium. In fact, every molecule of her body quivered. But her reaction gave her the momentum she needed to regain control of the situation. Unfortunately, she had the horrible suspicion she'd just leapt head-long from the frying pan into the fire.

"Turn around and keep walking, Mr. Wolffe," she said hoarsely. "We're leaving."

Dex had been as stunned by the contact of their bodies as she. At first he'd thought a robber had tailed him, intent on the wad of bills in his wallet. Now that he knew different, he still didn't want to turn as she'd commanded. He was paralyzed by the almost magnetic connection he felt. Though they'd had many verbal battles, this was only the second time he'd touched her. Obviously he'd had good reason not to—he wanted to kiss that defiant mouth of hers and never let it go.

He swallowed the urge with an effort, reminding himself who and what she was—a micro-managing corporate climber who'd catapulted through the ranks to within a single step of becoming chairman. At twenty-eight, she was the youngest, most powerful force in the banking industry. And, paradoxically, while he didn't believe the rumors of her sleeping her way to the top, he knew the stunning blonde had left her stiletto heel imprinted on backsides all over town. She must have studied at the Amber School of Business, he thought. She was an ambitious piranha—everything he detested in a human being—and he wanted to kiss her? He'd lose a lip if he tried.

"What's the matter?" he said with a sneer. "Is your broom in the shop for repairs?"

"Always so sure of yourself, aren't you?" Her chin tilted up. "Well, you went too far this time." She raised her wavering pocket and motioned him on. "You owe me, mister. Now move."

As she menaced him, he saw clearly the outline of her hand on the thin material, the knuckles that were bent around nothing but empty air. He blinked in disbelief.

The hard-nosed Miss Hamner was threatening him with her finger.

He choked on the bark of laughter that rose in his throat. And it wasn't only because of the comical overtones of the situation. Relief, sweet and strong, poured into him, though he didn't understand why. To top it off, he found himself absolving her for her little drama. It would never occur to her, of course to *ask* for a ride. Intrigued by her corny ploy, sensing she'd "kidnap" some other poor slob if he didn't comply, he decided to play along until he figured out why she'd resorted to this charade in the first place.

He led her to the far side of the garage. He'd parked away from the entrance to avoid any chance of marring the new white paint job he'd painstakingly done on his car.

He heard her footsteps falter, and glanced behind to find her staring, mouth open, at the long, low automobile. "Oh, hell," she murmured. "I wanted to avoid notice." She glared at him. "Only you would own a De Lorean."

"She's not a De Lorean," he told her, and unlocked his door. With a flourish, he pulled it up, instead of out. "But I think she's got a bit of that in her. This," he said, "is Sheila."

"Never heard of it," she said, eyeing it warily.

"That's not the make, it's her name." He stroked its sleek lines. "She was payment for a job I did last year. The guy designs his own cars." He smiled. "She's one of a kind."

"Thank God," she muttered, striding to the passenger side. Awkwardly clenching her purse, she reached for the handle. As she tugged, the door flew upward. She leaped back before it hit her on the head. "Your car hates me," she grumbled.

"It's a machine," he said. "No emotions."

She gave an unladylike snort. "A lot you know," she muttered, then hesitated when she saw the cluttered interior. "No maid service today?" she asked sweetly.

"Would you rather walk?" he returned in an equally saccharine tone.

"No." For a moment their gazes met through the window, releasing a surge of electricity inside her that defied logic. Then she brushed the offending newspapers to the floor, tossed her purse inside, and sat, her hand firmly in her pocket. He stripped off his glasses and set them on the dashboard.

"Don't you need those to see?"

"Only to read." He reached for the ignition key.

"Wait!" she cried, staring at the floor.

He narrowed his gaze, and for an instant he thought he saw a flash of something in those clear, Lauren Bacall eyes that didn't belong. Fear? From the Hammer?

Before he could be sure, she began to shuffle through the trash with the toes of her shoes. She smiled when she found fabric. Eagerly she snatched it up, forgetting her "gun" as she grabbed a filthy coverall with both hands. "Perfect," she said.

"For what?" he asked, confused.

"Never mind." She turned and peeled off her coat in a single fluid movement.

Dex watched her closely. Every movement she made was smooth and controlled, unintentionally enticing as the burgundy suit clung to every curve and contour. He could find her quite magnificent, if he liked her kind of woman.

He didn't, of course, he told himself quickly. That went without saying. But he had the oddest feeling that he was glimpsing the real woman beneath the uptight, buttoned-down corporate image. Though he trusted his instincts, he didn't like the implications.

"What are you doing?" he asked.

"If you had half the brain you think you have," she told him, "you'd figure it out." She kicked off her shoes, stuck her legs into the coverall, and zipped it over her suit.

He sighed. Then again, maybe it was his imagination after all. Maybe she'd simply broken under the pressure.

After shoving her pumps and her raincoat beneath the seat, she grabbed a battered Peterbilt hat and stuck it on her head. Then, smiling grimly, she reached for his glasses and wrapped the stems around her ears. "Dexter Wolffe," she said, "meet Fred, your mechanic."

He grimaced. "You must be kidding."

"I never kid. I'm in charge of this—" Her eyes widened. In an ostentatious show, she retrieved her coat and turned a shoulder to him to hide the transfer of the "gun" to the shapeless coverall's pocket. "It's time to leave now."

He started the engine, stifling a smile. She was either the worst criminal he'd ever seen, or she was desperate.

The word rebounded through his mind, twittering all sorts of little subconscious clues he'd been chasing ever since the Feds took him off the case. But he still couldn't define them.

As he drove toward the entrance, though, he realized what had prompted her elaborate ruse. Despite the inclement weather, reporters swarmed beyond the gate. Elizabeth slouched lower in her seat, pulled the brim of her hat down, and crossed her arms. As he showed his stub to the gate guard, the man glanced inside. She yawned and scratched her armpit.

Dex bit his lip to keep from laughing aloud. He'd never imagined her to be such a consummate actress! He rolled up his window and exited the lot, but she continued the performance as they passed the cameras. "It's not really necessary," he whispered as the reporters shoved microphones impotently toward the car. "In case you hadn't noticed, the glass is smoked. For all they know, Princess Diana could be in here."

Her chin went up again. "I knew that. I was just—I was merely—" The engine sputtered. "Don't stop."

"I wouldn't dare." He turned on the wipers and downshifted. Sheila balked. "She needs servicing," he explained as he accelerated.

"She needs an attitude adjustment," she said sourly.

He refused to get into a discussion about the quirks of a rebuilt engine. He had more pressing matters to deal with. "Where are we going?"

"Just drive," she said tersely.

"In which direction?" he asked.

"East. The airport. San Jose, Mr. Wolffe, not San Francisco."

She's going after her witness, he realized. True to form after all, she couldn't allow the authorities to handle the case. But a part of him couldn't blame her. He might think that finding Jane was a long shot, but Elizabeth probably thought it her only hope.

One corner of his mouth lifted. "You might as well call me Dex, Elizabeth. All my kidnappers do."

She turned to stare stubbornly out the rain-streaked window. "No. Just be quiet and drive."

He sighed. His concentration was not fully on the slick road. It was on her innocence, the reasons behind his certainty, and the knowledge that she was making the biggest mistake of her life with her wild-goose chase. His mind whirled as it sorted through the facts, sifting beneath them to find the truth.

For nearly an hour he struggled to find the clue he'd overlooked, but it was like trying to find a single grain of sand on the beach. As they passed the San Francisco airport, less than forty minutes from their destination, he drew a deep breath and let it go. Something was still missing. But he knew without a shadow of a doubt that somewhere in his research he'd found the proof they both needed. He simply had no idea of where—or what—it was.

Yet.

He glanced at her profile, silhouetted in the half-light of the storm. It was elegant and strong, as always, but it seemed to have a wistful quality he'd never noticed before. Her full mouth, usually set in tight lines, was relaxed, her blue eyes unfocused instead of laserlike. As he watched, she drew in her bottom lip and nibbled on it.

He focused his attention to the freeway ahead, firmly telling himself to quit thinking of her lithe figure, of the long legs that had been created to wrap around a man's body. He wanted nothing to do with a devious corporate woman again.

But he couldn't avoid his inborn curiosity. From the corner of his eye, he saw her sort through the contents of her purse and frown at a slip of paper. Blinking rapidly, she returned to her study of the raindrops, letting the paper drift to her lap.

Intuitively he knew this was her real motivation for the whole escapade. Squinting to make out the message in the gloom, he leaned closer. The neatly typed words fairly leaped from the page. He wished they hadn't.

"Death before dishonor," it read. "One way or another, the Hammer will surely fall."

His grip on the steering wheel tightened, his heart twisted in his chest. He wanted to strangle his parents for the weird mix of genes that had given him his instinctive analytical abilities, but especially for the upbringing that wouldn't let him ignore a woman in trouble, even this one. He wanted to groan aloud, to curse the Fates, his soft spot for underdogs, and every blasted emotion that conspired against his better judgment. Because Elizabeth didn't need just a witness.

She needed a protector.

His gaze narrowed on her in the murky, rain-induced gloom. She wasn't going to like his next move at all, but he had to trust his instincts.

He drove straight past the correct exit.

She didn't notice immediately, caught up in her study of the rain. They drove in stony silence for several wet miles before he saw her stiffen. "Where are you going?" she asked in a low, menacing tone.

Bracing himself for a storm that would make the late winter tempest outside seem like a light mist, Dex calmly said, "Phoenix."

Two

Elizabeth's throat tightened. Dammit, she knew it was a mistake to drop her guard with this sneaky, conniving tyrant! She shoved her hand in her pocket. "Turn around. Now."

He chuckled. "Come off it, Elizabeth. The only thing you can shoot with that is fingernail polish." He enunciated clearly. "A Beretta is a very big weapon."

Feeling completely demoralized, she drew herself up. "You *knew*," she cried. "Dammit, all this time you knew everything! You were—you son of a—" She stammered to a halt, unable to voice the entire litany of epithets in her brain. "Stop this car!"

"No. We're going to Phoenix, and we're going to clear your name."

"I don't need your help. I don't need anybody's help." To her fury, tears stung her eyes. Refusing to give in to them, or to the stubborn man beside her, she reached for the door handle and tugged.

"What are you doing?" he yelled.

"I'm not staying, that's for sure." She tugged again and shoved the door against the force of the wind. It cracked open. Cold air whooshed in, shooting up the loose leg of the coverall. The hissing tires became a thrum. Elizabeth glanced down at the pavement rushing beneath her and shuddered, but she couldn't back down now. Tearing her gaze away from the terrifying evidence of their speed, she glared at him. "One way or another, Mr. Wolffe, I'm leaving this car!"

He glared back, obviously debating whether or not to call her bluff. She raised her chin and eased the door upward another inch.

He lunged for her, but his attention was on the road, and she evaded him easily. "You're crazy!" he cried in astonishment.

"Yeah, I'm crazy! Crazy to have thought you had any honor!"

His jaw tightened. She reached for her seat belt.

With a fluency she hadn't heard since her father had been a drill instructor, Dex began to swear. Without pausing for breath, he yanked the wheel and bounded onto the shoulder. Her door popped open, then slammed shut at the sharp movement, catching her pant leg. The car bounced over the gravel, and, despite her restraints, Elizabeth's head hit the low ceiling. She blinked the stars from her vision as the car skidded to a halt.

After taking a deep breath, he swiveled toward her. "All right, get it out of your system."

She laughed mirthlessly. "We're not talking about a virus, Mr. Wolffe. I can't simply 'get it out of my system.'" She tried to spin toward him, but her pant leg was caught. Unobtrusively, she tugged at her knee. "You tricked me."

"And your little stunt doesn't constitute a trick?" He crossed his arms. "Besides, I thought you were interested in making a getaway."

She was stunned by his audacity. "Didn't it occur to you that I had my own plans? And that you were hardly included?"

"No," he said calmly. "You made it very clear that you needed me to get out of that building. If I hadn't been there, who knows what would have happened."

Her chin tilted up as his reminder hit home, and she glared down the length of her nose. "You're the reason I'm in this situation in the first place, Mr. Wolffe. Why would I possibly need you any further than the airport?"

"You need somebody, lady, that's for sure."

Her nostrils flared. "I don't need a cop!"

"I'm an independent—the police listen to me, not the other way around. I just found the evidence." He leaned forward. "This 'situation' is your fault, not mine."

"In case you've forgotten, I'm the victim here," she said.

"If you had been more careful with your security, the real criminal would have had trouble accessing your personal code."

"Your stupid system changed it every month!"

"And you probably wrote it down and slipped it into your desk!"

"I—you—" In some dim, reasonable part of her mind she admitted the truth of his words. Despising being put on the defensive, she jerked the handle. "I don't have to stay and listen to this garbage." She yanked and shoved, but the door remained stubbornly shut.

"Apparently you do," he said with a suspicious hint of amusement. "The lock is jammed."

"Then fix it!"

"No way. We're in the middle of nowhere, and you're a captive audience. You have to listen to me now." He reached for her hand, but she sat on it. He sighed. "You need to get to Phoenix, unseen by Feds and media, and I can get you there and back by morning." He nodded at her lap. "Why didn't you show that to Harry?"

She grabbed the forgotten note, clenching it in her fist. Why hadn't she left the damn thing in her purse? Had she wanted him to see it? Had the consummate loner somehow chosen an ally?

Frowning at the thought, she dropped her gaze to the crumpled sheet, battling to keep her animosity. "Give me a little credit, Mr. Wolffe. It's the third I've gotten this week. Standard office stationery, no fingerprints, untraceable." She gave a short laugh. "Everyone thinks I'm sending them to myself to divert suspicion." The confession surprised her.

His jaw tightened. "You and I know better. Someone is doing his best to make sure you take the fall for this embezzlement. I can't let that happen."

She stilled. "*You* can't let that happen," she repeated.

He smiled crookedly. "I have this thing about the unjustly accused. That's one reason I got out of the corporate world in the first place."

She tensed as his gaze drifted to the window, knowing there had to be more. "And?"

"And—" He lifted a shoulder. "Elizabeth, I designed the security program, so naturally I was called to find the problem. I found hundreds of thousands of dollars loaned to dummy corporations with your name all over every fake transaction, your terminal signature as the point of origin. I might be off the case, but I can't quit. I have to trace that money."

Of course, she thought, he believed her guilty. Dexter Wolffe would never fly to her aid without an ulterior motive. "So you figured, Hey! What better way to find the cash then to go to the source, right? To nab the culprit, let her hijack you. Maybe she'll spill the beans!" She couldn't admit how much that hurt—and frightened—her. If the real criminal was still planting false evidence against her, there was no doubt in her mind that Dexter would find the money all right—in her account.

He stifled a grin. "You watch a lot of old gangster movies, don't you?"

Her mouth firmed. "You're such a genius, you figure it out. I'm not going to stick around and let you crucify me." With muttered comments on his probable parentage, her opinion of cars, computers, and life in general, she heaved backward. The worn material at her thigh finally ripped, leaving her pant leg dangling from the edge of the door. But when she tried the handle, it still refused to budge.

"Why are you fighting me? I'm on your side!"

She wanted so much to believe him, to accept his help. But she'd spent too many years depending on no one but herself. "You're on nobody's side but your own," she said, a grunt escaping her as her hand slipped. "And your methods prove it. Lulling the criminal into a false sense of security is not only unoriginal, it's indecent."

He chuckled, firing her anger. She rolled down

the window, unbuckled her seat belt, and heaved herself to the wet edge of the opening. She ducked down to snag her purse and deliver her parting shot. "Enjoy your job, Mr. Wolffe. Sending innocent women to jail must be terribly satisfying."

And with that, she scooted through the window.

As she hit the ground, sharp gravel bit at the soles of her bare feet, the gale buffeted her body. She closed her eyes tightly and shuddered as she realized her shoes were still residing beneath her seat, and she'd managed to escape during the worst of the squall. When was she going to learn to plan ahead for her dramatic exits?

Breathing a silent prayer, she looked around, but saw no glimmer of civilization anywhere. She was surrounded by nothing but huge, ominous boulders and storm-slapped eucalyptus trees.

"Baby, it's cold out there," she heard over the howl of the wind.

Water poured down the back of her neck, increasing her discomfort, but she wouldn't give in. Squaring her shoulders, she started walking.

"Hey, Elizabeth," he called through his window, "get back in the car. I'm trying to help you, not send you to jail."

"Sure you are!" A rock bruised her heel, sending a siren of pain through her brain.

The car purred to life and crunched slowly toward her, catching her in its headlights. "Are you going to walk to Phoenix?"

She spun around, shouting over the roaring wind. "Yes! If I have to." She choked on a mouthful of rainwater and lowered her face, wiping her eyes clear. "Your conscience is clear. You don't have to help me. You don't even like me!"

"So?"

Her chest heaved, and she found that she was angrier that he hadn't denied it than about the sentiment itself. "I don't need you holding me back, Wolffe," she said in the voice of the Velvet Hammer. "I can move faster without worrying that my every move is being reported."

"I report to no one but myself," he said in a low, dangerous tone.

"So you can take all the credit."

Silence.

"Can't deny that, can you?" A fleeting memory of his earlier words filtered through her anger for an instant. Was she unjustly accusing him?

She shook off all emotion and stomped toward him, her feet now effectively numb to the gravel. She couldn't afford remorse or any other hindrance to her goal. "Get this and get it good, Mr. Wolffe. I've done fine on my own for my entire life. I'll be at the top of the corporate ladder by the time I'm thirty because I've worked hard and I've never asked anyone to do a job I can do myself. I'm not some pansy-faced piece of fluff who needs the protection of a big, strong man."

"Of course you'll be at the top," he countered. "You started halfway up!"

She'd heard all the taunts before and she refused to dignify them with an answer. "Despite what you obviously think of me, I've lived in places you wouldn't keep a dog in. I've been up at dawn working my buns off, and loved every minute of it. You want to play Lone Ranger and rescue a maiden in distress"—she gave the car a brief look of disgust—"get a horse!"

Elizabeth stubbed her toe on a rock the size of

Rhode Island and dropped her purse, ruining the effect her brave words had created. Knowing he could see every move clearly, she bent for it quickly and slapped it on her thigh. Imagining his laughter, she lifted her chin and glared at him. She didn't need his help, she thought, but thanks to his interference, she needed his car. Clenching her fists, she shivered as her obstinate pride fought with her common sense.

Dex watched her silent debate with herself. Unfortunately, his thoughts were no less riotous. In the last few hours he'd defied the urgings of logic, aided and abetted a possible felon, and, worse yet, allowed his emotions and his chivalry to cloud his judgment. His instincts told him Elizabeth Hamner was innocent, that he needed to protect her. Fine. He should've locked her in his house and glued himself to her terminal, not hared off into the wild West! But now that he'd committed himself, he couldn't abandon her.

After a moment, she hobbled to his side. He lowered the window. Rain trickled down her face. Her blue eyes clouded with hurt and stubborn anger, daring him to explain himself.

But he sensed something beneath the obvious emotion—the same glimmer of fear he'd glimpsed in San Francisco—and he felt a cold sweat break out on his brow. After seeing nothing but her confidence and acidic temper for two years, this carefully hidden flicker made her a hundred times more vulnerable—and more beautiful—than any woman he'd ever known, simply because she pressed on in spite of it.

Clearing his throat, he realized he was in dangerous territory. If he began believing his musings were more than wishful thinking, he would be in deep trouble. As the rain seeped through the window, he finally asked, "Well? Are you going to get in the car or do you want to throw another tantrum?"

An eighteen-wheeled monster roared by and caught her in the backwash. Gallons of water hit her square in the derriere, and the excess doused him through the window. With a shriek, Elizabeth bolted to the passenger side and yanked at the handle.

"It won't open!" she cried.

Wiping his face on his sleeve, Dex leaned over and jerked the handle.

The door burst open, hitting Elizabeth's knee. Hopping mad—literally—she tossed her purse behind her seat, leaped into the car, and slammed the door. Dripping all over the upholstery, she glared at his stifled grin. "I told you she hates me."

"Pure coincidence," he told her.

Elizabeth gave an unladylike snort. "I should have taken the hint and stayed away from you. But I guess I can't now, can I?"

He realized he'd been holding his breath. "You've decided to stay?"

"Do I have a choice?"

"No."

"Then you have a passenger, don't you."

"Good." Wondering if what he felt was relief or sheer panic, he shoved the car into gear and eased it back onto the freeway.

Within minutes they had traveled out of the center of the storm into its drizzly edges. In the gray, misty light, he had his first good look at Elizabeth.

He glanced at her soaked, one-legged jumpsuit, at her bedraggled hair, and he choked on a spurt of laughter. The corporate clone had been dragged backward through a dirty wind tunnel, he decided. "The first time I saw you," he said unsteadily, "I thought you looked like a lioness or a tigress or one of the other aristocratic felines." He bit his lip. "Now you look almost human."

"You're not in much better shape, buster."

Their gazes met. Blue entwined with gray, then her mouth trembled and a giggle burst through.

He'd never heard her laugh, he suddenly realized. The sound reminded him of a clear brook, babbling merrily over worn stones. Almost embarrassed, she broke contact first, her laughter slowing, then disappearing.

His gaze dropped to her feet, and the shredded panty hose.

Despite his amusement, his heart caught somewhere in his throat when he realized the damage she'd done to herself. Next time he'd remember the extent of her stubborn determination. "Take off your clothes," he said.

"I won't take—"

"There's a blanket shoved behind you somewhere," he went on, "and a first aid kit under the seat." When she didn't move, he softened his harsh tone. "If you sit in those wet clothes, Beth, you'll catch pneumonia."

"I won't—" She drew in a breath. "*What* did you call me?"

He blinked, startled himself, but the name fit her. Very dangerous territory, he thought. "Miss

Hamner, please do us both a favor and strip. I would hate to have to take you to the hospital."

She hesitated, the intimacy of the car's interior suddenly making her nervous. If only he'd stop looking at her that way . . .

"Don't worry," he told her teasingly. "I'll control myself."

She felt ridiculous for imagining Dexter would ever find her attractive. She'd learned the hard way that men usually admired her only for her business acumen. They rarely related to her on any other level. But somewhere deep down inside she'd thought Dexter Wolffe was different.

She tossed her head, sending drops of water and bobby pins flying. "Could you turn on the heater?" she asked, deciding it was smart to focus on pulling herself together.

"Making the best of it, eh?" Dex said.

"Why am I always the one to make the best of bad situations?" she grumbled.

"Maybe because you get yourself into them so often."

She reached for the oil-stained wool blanket. Grimacing, she held it up by two fingers. "It appears that you've been wiping Sheila's nose with this."

"Only when it leaks."

She gave him a dark look and wrapped it around herself, fumbling with her clothing beneath. "Just don't call me 'Beth' again," she muttered. "You might as well choose 'Princess' or 'Kitten' or one of those other nauseating nicknames."

He didn't stifle his grin this time. "Okay, Princess Kitten."

She froze, then unzipped the coverall and

slipped it down her legs. "I take it back. Elizabeth will do nicely." She smiled sweetly. "And I'll call you Spiderman."

"What?" Startled, since he hadn't heard that name in years, he glanced at her. "Why do you say that?"

"Your ring. Or is that squiggly thing an octopus?" She wrinkled her nose. "No, you're definitely a spider." She slanted a look through her lashes. "Sneaky, predatory, and a builder of complex webs."

"Actually, they used to call me that because of my instincts." He shook his head. "They thought I had the comic-book hero's sixth sense for danger, but, in actuality, I was always able to piece together fragments of information with almost no thought at all. I just think faster than anyone else."

Unwilling to admit the explanation intrigued her, she held up the ragged jumpsuit. "Where should I put this?"

He shrugged. "Toss it behind you."

She did, then gave him a dry smile. "I'm not going to find Jimmy Hoffa, am I?"

"No comments about the housekeeping, please. Don't forget who's driving."

"Geez, touchy, touchy." She twisted around to drape her jacket over the back of her seat.

The blanket split up her thigh, and she quickly tugged it closed, but not before he caught a glimpse of garter. Stockings, he realized. The shark didn't wear panty hose, she wore lingerie. Warmth pooled in various parts of his body at the thought of what else lay under the ratty wool envelope.

He cleared his throat abruptly, forcing his

thoughts away from the titillating peep show. He didn't want that kind of relationship with her. He'd had his fill of corporate women ten years before, when he'd been used as a rung in Amber's climb to the top. Hell, he thought, he'd been her ladder! If he couldn't convince his contrary instincts that Elizabeth Hamner and Amber were two rotten peas in a pod, this trip would be pure agony.

"I have a theory," he announced, concentrating on the flicker of streetlights ahead. They were nearing a town. He wished his peripheral vision was nonexistent, or that another front would blow in.

"About what?" she asked, contorting into an impossible position to slip her blouse over her head. She laid it over her jacket. "The embezzlement?"

His knuckles whitened on the steering wheel. If he'd been wearing his glasses, they'd have melted by now. Not even the fact that his sweater was damp, too, distracted him from the impossible length of leg that the blanket didn't begin to conceal. "The embezzlement," he repeated, priming the pump. "Yes, the embezzlement." What had he begun to say? "The—the executives. Your colleagues. The five others."

"Of course it's one of them." She carefully folded the skirt and set it atop her purse, just behind her. "So tell me, why do *you* think the criminal isn't a stranger?"

He swallowed hard as his imagination began to draw vivid pictures of what was left on her body. "The pattern's all wrong," he heard himself say, grateful that part of his mind was still functioning normally. "The criminal knew the inner workings of the bank," he went on, "and at a very high level. And something keeps bugging me about those dummy corporations."

"What?"

"If I knew, we wouldn't be driving down a road in the middle of nowhere." He shook off the recurring thought. It would come to him if he didn't focus on it. "Besides, no outsider could have gotten through my security system."

"I love modesty in a man," she muttered.

"So," he went on, ignoring her comment, "who resents you enough to frame you for embezzlement?"

"They all do," she said promptly, without remorse.

"I wonder why?" he murmured.

Her chin firmed. "I've made a few enemies, I'll admit it. But it's because I don't play their games."

Her denial worked like a splash of cold water, since he knew better. It didn't quite erase his arousal, but it was a start. He didn't want to like her! "Don't give me that. I know all about you, Elizabeth Hamner. Father in the Marines, only child, graduated from Yale." He might have been reciting Amber's history. He needed to remind himself not to trust Elizabeth. "Isn't it strange that your CEO is an ex-Marine officer who also happened to go to Yale?"

"Just what are you implying?" she asked in a frosty tone.

"You didn't earn that job. You used your connections and walked right into it."

She nodded. "I should have known you were setting me up." She spun toward him, her ice-blue eyes blazing. "Two years ago you treated all of us as if our heads were filled with straw. Now you're twisting the facts around to justify this superior and oh-so-condescending manner of yours. I'm sick of it!" She jabbed him in the shoulder. "At least I have a college education."

He tensed. "Is it a crime not to?"

She poked him again. "What's wrong? Can't admit that you're not perfect? Well, let me tell you a few things from *my* point of view." She ticked them off on her fingers, clutching the drooping blanket with her elbows. "You were let go—" she coughed, a sound of sarcasm, not illness—"excuse me, you quit the only real job you ever had. For the last ten years you've been free-lancing and currently have no credit record, and no real assets to speak of." She gave the car a dirty look. "Your bank accounts add up to under a thousand dollars, and you work only when you need rent money." She sneered. "You think I walked into my job—you threw yours away!"

"You've been a busy little bee," he said, relaxing when he realized she didn't know the whole story. If she'd heard more than rumor, if she knew he'd been foolish enough to fall in love with a woman who'd stolen a vital program he'd created and labeled it her own, she would taunt him with it. In a way, he was grateful for her for the reminder that corporate women were treacherous. "But you've neglected a few things."

"Such as?"

Noticing a familiar, luminous sign for a convenience store, he eased onto an exit ramp. Since he couldn't quite keep his mind off her nearly naked body, he needed certain items to preserve his sanity. "First of all, they tried to hire me straight out of high school. I, uh, had a reputation."

"I'll bet you did. What did you do? Follow the leader and hack your way into the defense computers?"

"Not quite." He smiled grimly. He didn't usually blow his own horn, but she had to learn not to jump to conclusions. "When my father balanced the books, he'd come up one cent short. He figured it was subtraction errors, but I saw a pattern. For nearly a year, every month, one penny missing." He shrugged. "I had a 'hacker' friend . . . which, by the way, is a compliment to some people"—her sulky expression told him she hadn't known—"and I used his computer to get into the bank's. I remember thinking it was too easy, that technology had leapt far ahead of the law, as usual. Then I found it."

She gasped, muttering a curse. He grinned. She knew where he was leading now, and it irritated her. He wouldn't deny himself the pleasure of delivering the final blow. "Imagine my surprise when I found that every other account on the national network was being methodically drained of one cent each and every month. Quite a little scam, I'll tell you that. But it was a breeze to put a tracer on it. He wasn't *that* good." He eased into the parking lot and switched off the engine, frowning as he feigned a faulty memory. "How much did they eventually decide he stole?"

She mumbled something.

"What? I didn't hear you."

She shot him a venomous glare. "Three million dollars." She ran an impatient hand through her hair, dislodging the few remaining hairpins. "But—"

He opened his door. "And I did go to one semester at Stanford, on a football scholarship, but I grew ten inches that year." He leaned back in to whisper, "Ruined my knees. Some of us couldn't afford fancy colleges without a rich daddy or friends on the Board of Regents." He straightened. "While I'm inside, use the first aid kit on those feet!"

As he slammed the door, Elizabeth's indignation rose. That was it? A parting shot and the conversation was over, with no chance of retaliation? She began to climb out of the car, realized she'd be arrested for indecent exposure, and rolled down her window instead. Vaguely, she noticed the rain had stopped. "Where are you going?"

"You'll see!" he shouted as he retreated across the lot.

She sniffed. That's exactly what it was, she decided, a strategic retreat. When faced with superior forces, he retires, the apparent victor, with a crack and a command.

But she had to smile. At least she'd made her point, and without any maudlin explanations. Just as she'd known only half his story, he knew only bits and pieces of hers too. The question was would he admit it?

She shrugged, deciding she shouldn't care. She disliked him and he disliked her. They were merely using each other to reach their own goals, and she thoroughly trounced the part of her heart that cried out at the thought. It was a perfect, uncomplicated relationship as far as she was concerned, much better than that strange, magnetic pull she'd felt while she'd undressed. Only stupid romantic fools wept over what might have been. And she was hardly one of them.

By the time he returned and tossed a heavy bag in her lap, she'd managed to rationalize herself into a passable mood. "What's this?" she asked.

"Open it."

"Nothing's going to jump out at me, is it?"

He groaned. "Lord, you have a suspicious mind."

"I figured you might pay me back for the little lesson in humility," she told him calmly.

He turned toward her. "Okay, I'll admit it. I *did* jump to a few conclusions myself. Why don't you clear them up for me?"

"I don't think so," she said, smiling. "Letting too much hot air out of that ego might shock your system into total shutdown. As long as you can admit there's another side, that's good enough for me."

He reached beneath her seat to pull out a rectangular box. "Just making sure I returned the favor."

"You didn't have to." She jumped when he grasped her ankles and yanked her feet over the stick shift. The sack in her lap slid to the littered floor. As her neck twisted and her head slid down the window, she gasped out a curse, but he ignored her. She flushed as the blanket gaped open, revealing her camisole, panties, and garter in all their splendor.

"I—um." He cleared his throat. "I've got to do something about that heater," he muttered. His fingers caressed her leg, but his gaze was definitely on her breasts.

She glanced at the rock-hard buds protruding

from the silk, then at his half-lidded gray eyes. A liquid spasm of warmth puddled in her middle, spreading through her limbs with electric speed. "What are you doing?" she managed to ask.

He visibly shook himself. "I told you to bandage those feet." Hesitating only briefly, Dex twitched the scanty covering closed and wrenched up the lid of the first aid kit, his touch impersonal. "I don't want you getting an infection."

"I'm never sick," she said, irritated. She was reacting to his touch like a sex-starved teenager, and he looked at her as if she were an interesting specimen of fungus. She must have imagined the hunger, the brief throb of a desire her idiotic body had echoed. Throb, she thought in disgust; it was more like a hiccup!

He dabbed antiseptic on the abrasions. She hissed as it bit into her sole and decided she needed a distraction—from the feel of his hands on her as much as from the sting. She groped for the bag and pulled out the topmost item, a hairbrush. "Is this a hint?"

He shrugged and unrolled gauze. "It's either that or some poor bird will call you 'home.'"

She glanced at his own shaggy style. "And what makes you an expert, Mr. Lawn Mowers Are Us?"

He acknowledged her hit with a tilt of his head. "You might as well bring the rest of it out."

Warily, she extracted the articles—a pair of jeans, two flip-flops for her abused feet, and a black T-shirt. This she held up by the shoulders, stifling a gasp at the slogan. "Cute," she muttered, and turned it toward him, not an easy maneuver in her semi-reclining position. "'Die Yuppie Scum,'" she read, nodding. "Uh-huh."

"Couldn't resist." He grinned and wrapped her wounds securely. "None of the cuts were deep," he said as he tossed the remaining bandages into the kit. "But keep an eye on them."

"Yes, doctor." She straightened, realizing she did feel better. "Now what?"

He switched on the engine. It sputtered, he pounded the dashboard, and it wheezed to life. "Feed Sheila," he said, ignoring the foibles of his car as they wheeled into the nearby gas station.

She slipped the T-shirt over her head, hiding her smile. They were back on familiar ground as cheerful adversaries, and that was an alliance she could handle.

As long as they remained on equal footing—so to speak—she could retain her command and hold all of her problems at bay, including this disturbing chemistry.

As they eased next to a pump, she reached around for her purse. "I pay my own way," she told him firmly. "For the gas, the clothes, the bandages, and anything else."

He shrugged and went to fill the tank. "I'm not arguing."

She opened the flap of the purse and peered inside. Then, her heart pounding, she searched through its meager contents—lip gloss, mascara, two ballpoint pens, and the prescription refill she'd picked up that morning. But she saw no sign of the bulky, tan wallet.

With a curse, she bounded to her knees and began to toss clothes, trash, and felt-tip markers around the car. "Dammit!" she said when she found only the usual clutter.

She patted the pockets of her jacket, praying she'd slipped it into one. Nothing but dampness.

She went cold as she remembered. Damp. Rain. Dropping her purse in the gravel. "Oh, great," she whispered, and sunk her head to her hands, kicking herself mentally. Why had she agreed to this lunacy? And why, oh, why couldn't she have lost something a little less important, like her birth control pills? Lord knew she would hardly need *those* this trip!

Dex stuck his head through the window. "Find it?"

"No!" she wailed. "I think it's in a gully somewhere south of San Jose."

"It's okay, I have money."

How could she tell him he'd missed the point completely? Her world was crumbling around her again, and she had absolutely no control over it! Where was her strong-willed resolution when she needed it?

"It—it's not just the money." She swallowed. Dammit, she would not fall apart, especially in front of him! "My credit cards, checkbook, everything was in there."

"See what happens when you depend on those little pieces of plastic?" he said smugly.

She groaned. "Oh, Lord, he doesn't carry credit cards, either."

"We're only going to be gone twenty-four hours," he pointed out. "We'll survive."

She drew a deep, shuddering breath. "That's not all. Jane's unlisted phone number and her address are gone too."

"Then let's go back," he said, taking her hand in his. "I thought this was a long shot from the beginning. There are more reliable ways of clearing you, and I could put you somewhere safe from whoever is threatening you."

Her fingers trembled. His concern was palpable, his touch as comforting as a favorite teddy bear, yet the heat that flared between them made her think of more things to do in bed than sleep.

She shivered, realizing that Dexter Wolffe in close quarters was more dangerous than the police, the Feds, and the real criminal rolled into one. And if she didn't pull herself together, if she couldn't regain her authority, who knew where it would end?

Resolutely, she withdrew her hand. "No. I can't go back, and it's not because of those notes—none of my colleagues would ever follow through on them anyway." She straightened her shoulders. "And we have plenty of time for your research on the way to Phoenix."

"You never know, we might actually find something by then." He pulled out of the station. "Look at it this way—everything that could go wrong has." He shrugged. "Why worry, right?"

She slipped into her jeans. "Right."

Three

Elizabeth gazed out over the craggy horizon that shimmered in the afternoon sunlight. At least, she thought it did. At the moment, obscured by the haze of steam spitting from Sheila's radiator, it could be purple with red stripes for all she knew.

Dex leaned into the engine, his sweater sleeves pushed up, his features creased in what she'd begun to think of as his "problem-solving" expression. She'd seen that look too many times in the last twenty-four hours.

Elizabeth sighed, stretching her legs out the open doorway. "'Why worry?'" she mocked softly, and rolled her eyes heavenward. "Congratulations on smacking some of that arrogant certainty out of him, but couldn't You have found a better method?"

Running roughened fingers through her hair, she sighed again, wondering what had possessed her to agree to this lunacy. She should have kept walking until she'd reached San Jose!

When the car died in Buttonwillow, Elizabeth hadn't said a word. When their tire blew in Bakersfield, she'd gritted her teeth and endured. Even after dawn was long behind them and they still hadn't cleared California, she'd simply narrowed her eyes on the stretch of road before them and visualized Sheila in a giant trash compactor—with Dexter Wolffe sitting in the driver's seat. Elizabeth had no creative vengeance left in her. She was too hungry, too tired, and, she privately admitted, too damned worried.

Unable to sit passively by, she walked over to Dex. She peered around his arm. He glanced at her and stared, his gray eyes void of expression. Reminded of who had mistakenly snapped the key connection on the distributor cap in Barstow, she shoved her grease-stained hands in her back pockets and stepped away. He returned to the engine.

She rocked from foot to foot, wishing he would stop giving her the silent treatment and wondering if sunstroke was as slow and horrible a death as she'd heard. "How far are we from Phoenix?"

"Not counting this delay, or should I factor that in?"

"Take a guess."

"Three hours plus. But if Jane's bank closes at five, we won't make it."

Concerned that they wouldn't find her there, stung by his cavalier attitude, she said, "You can't fix this, can you." It wasn't a question. His implication that a three-hour drive would take five was enough.

Deliberately, he went to the driver's side and wiped his hands on a rag. "If I can't find water, it will take too long to cool the radiator down," he said finally, then straightened and studied their barren surroundings.

She swore. "The nearest gas station is ten miles behind us." Across the driest, most desolate wasteland she'd ever seen, she thought. Yesterday she'd cursed the rain. Now she'd give her left arm for a single cloud! Dammit, why was this happening to her? "Any bright ideas, Spiderman?"

"Well, I could remind you that it was your idea to take this godforsaken route to save time, or—"

"Mine! Who wanted to avoid Los Angeles?"

He ignored the reminder and nodded down the road, shoving his door closed. "—or we can check out that flash beside that camel-shaped rock. It's only about two miles up, and it looks like a building of some sort." Without even looking back, he started walking.

Every horrible epithet Elizabeth could think of sprang immediately to mind, but her lack of saliva prevented her from voicing any. The thought of water sucked at her mouth like a vacuum cleaner. Irritably, she yanked the tube of lip balm from her useless purse, applied it lavishly, then slammed her door, content in the knowledge that he was twice as miserable in his cable-knit sweater.

As if reading her thoughts, he shimmied it off and draped it over his head.

She shoved the gloss into her pocket and trailed after him, her thongs barely protecting her still-tender feet from the sharp gravel lining the road's shoulder. He looked ridiculous, she thought spitefully.

It took her less than a minute to realize he had the right idea. The merciless sun at its zenith drilled through her skull. With a mental curse she thought of the Peterbilt cap, still on the car's cluttered floor, and swiveled to look behind her. Already Sheila seemed miles away. And Dex still trudged ahead. She set her jaw. If he could make it, then, dammit, so could she!

Despite herself, her gaze traveled over him as he walked. She'd never seen him without a shirt on, and it hadn't occurred to her that he had such a wide expanse of tanned muscle hiding under there. She searched for fat or disfiguring scars—any kind of flaw would do!—but she saw nothing but smooth, sun-browned skin covering solid sinew and bone. When her gaze followed the tapering waist downward, her foolish feminine mind whistled in appreciation. Long legs and a tight, flat bottom would make any woman drool, she rationalized, at least if she had anything to drool with!

No, she told herself firmly. She would *not* fall into that trap! She was in complete control of the situation. And she didn't even *like* Dexter Wolffe. He was arrogant, boorish, and lazy. He didn't even work more than once a year! They had absolutely nothing in common.

So? whispered the feminine side.

Shut up, snapped the executive.

Distracted by her internal debate, dizzy and nauseous from the sun, she didn't notice when the road ended and the driveway began. She didn't hear the ghostly strains of music or smell the telltale wood smoke. When Dex stopped, she bumped into him, nose-first, dead on the point between his shoulder blades where she'd decided a knife would do the most good. Startled, she skipped away with a muttered apology, then scanned the building.

She blinked at the huge, distinctive half-cylinder of sheet tin, dulled by years and the shade of the butte. The last time she'd seen anything like it, there had been rows of them stretching across a Marine base. "What's a Quonset hut doing in the middle of nowhere?" she wondered aloud, puzzled.

Dex pointed to a hand-painted placard that read, "Danny's Bar and Grill. Last stop before Sawdi-land."

She frowned. "Okay," she corrected, "what's a Quonset hut with a misspelled sign doing in the mid—" She cut herself off, tossing her head back to sniff, and nearly fainting as she recognized the scent. "Ribs," she said in the soulful voice of one who'd had too many fast-food burgers too long ago. Without a backward glance, she shoved past him through the wooden door.

"Wait—" he called.

"Not on your life!" Inside, she halted abruptly, disoriented by the dark, smoky interior. Vaguely she realized that all conversation had hushed, that only the sound of Reba McEntire filled the room, but her painful, growling stomach was incentive enough to spur her on. And when the odor of beer reached her, she gripped her middle to keep from doubling over. Heaven, she was in heaven!

"Didn't you see the trucks?" asked Dex in her ear.

"What trucks?" She sighed.

"The troop carriers?"

"The—" Her vision adjusted with a click. She saw a long, wooden bar running the length of the left side, with neon signs advertising brands of beer and soda. She saw several tables dotting the planked floor, with four chairs around each. She saw the pinball machine, the pool table to the right, and two decimated dartboards stuck to the dented wall. She saw the proprietor, standing gaping behind the bar.

And she saw the men, all twenty or thirty of them . . . all with necks like tree trunks and all staring at her as if they were starving hyenas.

"Had enough?" he asked.

Nothing short of a mortar round was going to budge her now, not with the promise of barbecue and his smug question goading her. Besides, she'd recognized the insignias on their tan, camouflage fatigues.

"They're Marines," she said, "the most courteous, most decent bunch of men ever to grace the military."

With a fearful howl, the biggest one slammed his head to his table. The wood splintered, then fell into two neat pieces.

Dex gave her a dry look. She shrugged. "Okay, they're animals." Unnerved, she glanced around, feeling like a chocolate pastry at a Weight Watchers convention. "I wonder what they're doing here in the middle of the afternoon."

"I'll ask." He started forward.

She caught his arm. "It doesn't matter."

"Want to wait outside?" he asked with his mocking grin.

"No way. Do you?" When he shook his head, she nodded and looked around again. Steeling herself, she stepped into the room. The men at the three tables ahead of her stood and held their chairs. She turned. Two more tables cleared. With a sigh, she strode to the one nearest the door, thanking the lance corporal who seated her. The owner brought water, coffee, and menus. Eagerly, she downed the former.

"Hey, sip it, sip it!" Dex cried. "You're going to make yourself sick!"

Her stomach roiled, and she knew it was her current predicament that had knotted it. Not the bar, of course—she could handle a bunch of Marines. It was Jane's unnerving disappearance. Even she had to admit it wasn't a matter of lousy circumstance anymore, of making the best of a bad situation. Something was wrong. Very wrong. "Jane should have been at work when I called," she said softly.

He slid a menu over to her, frowning. "Maybe you mixed up the days."

"She always comes back from her vacation on a Thursday. Always." Elizabeth brought the coffee to her lips, caught the strong aroma, and set it down, shuddering. "She—she detests the mountain of paperwork and the"—she swallowed hard—"the long work week waiting for her." She buried her oil-stained fingers in her hair. "Dammit, why did she pick now to get irresponsible?"

"What if the Feds followed up on her after all? What if she wasn't there because they'd taken her back to San Francisco?"

"And maybe little green men swooped her up in their spaceship," she said with a mirthless laugh.

"Maybe she reconciled with her ex-husband and ran off to Tibet."

Elizabeth shook her head, feeling sweat pop out on her brow. "She's scared to death of her ex-husband. She's an expert at running away from him." She gritted her teeth against the pain of her stinging stomach. "Any way you look at it, if I can't find her, I'm dead."

"Don't worry, Beth. It doesn't matter if we can't. We'll find a way to figure out the key to my research."

She couldn't even manage a nasty comment.

"Beth? Dammit, I told you to sip it. Are you all right?"

Elizabeth clenched her fists. She shouldn't have gulped her water, but, dammit, she hated it when he was right! The dizziness had passed, but she hung on to her frayed temper for dear life. "Oh, I'm just peachy," she muttered, sagging in her chair. "My freedom is riding on the man who fingered me, the capricious schedule of an unreliable divorcée, and the whims of a neurotic hybrid sports car who obviously hates my guts. What could possibly be wrong?"

"Sheila doesn't hate your guts," he said, his mouth quivering with repressed laughter.

Her head snapped up. "No? Thanks to that mechanical monstrosity I know more about engines than Henry Ford and I can change a tire in hundred-degree heat without breaking a sweat."

He spread his hands wide. "See? It's a learning experience."

She picked a wisp of blonde hair out of her lopsided fingernail, cursing the fact that her file had disappeared with her wallet. "You sound just like my father." She rubbed her aching neck. "If I didn't hurt all over, I'd show you a learning experience you'd never forget."

He sipped his coffee. "Maybe we should go over the list of suspects again."

"If I hear their names one more time, they'll find little pieces of you all over the bar," she said with a growl. "We're not going to find anything new in that pile of sexist laundry. My only hope is to get Jane back to San Francisco!"

He smiled and scanned his laminated menu. "You're like a dog with a bone, aren't you?"

"Me? Who grilled whom last night until I was ready to scream? I told you a thousand times—I don't know anything more about them, consciously or subconsciously! They're all properly married with tidy little executive families! I don't know if they gamble, I don't know if they have Swiss bank accounts, and they *all* resent me enough to frame me for a multimillion-dollar embezzlement!"

"You remembered Nigel is allergic to shellfish and that Wayne is a killer racquetball player," he said calmly.

She laughed. "Only because I went through an idiotic phase where I actually wanted to find things in common with them. I thought it would make my life easier if we all got along. It didn't work." Something flashed through her mind, but she said nothing. Not only was the information useless, but if she told him, she'd be giving in. And she never gave in. "Dammit, Dex, they could each have six wives in Alaska and dance naked in the moonlight, and I'd never know it!"

He peered over the menu. "It's nice to know you haven't lost your sense of humor."

She slapped the plastic menu to the table. "Don't push me, Spiderman. I'm filthy and I've had three hours' sleep in the last thirty-six—and that in a car parked in the middle of the desert. I look like something no self-respecting vulture would be interested in, I smell even worse, and I feel like Quasimodo's twin sister!"

He stared at her for a moment, then picked up the menu and returned to his perusal. "Make the best of it."

She rubbed her hands on her jeans, feeling the same trapped sensation she'd felt so often as a child. "When Dad was in Vietnam—tour after tour—I had to 'make the best of it.' When he came home and he was . . . different, and we moved every year, I still had to 'make the best of it.'" Her chin came up. "I'm tired of 'making the best of it.' I got where I am in the company by *not* making the best of it!"

He sighed. "Then bully right in as usual, Hammer, and good luck to you." He stood. "Get yourself into more trouble. Faint from starvation on the way. I'm going to order, and see if I can find a cure for Sheila's ills."

Subtly rebuked, Elizabeth turned away to stare at the flickering lights on the jukebox. The nickname stung coming from him, and it irritated her that she didn't know why. She'd heard it from other people hundreds of times, and it had never made her feel as if someone had smacked her hand away from the cookie jar.

Staring unseeing, she bit her lip and blinked back the moisture that formed in her eyes despite her best efforts. But inside she was coiled like Bruce Lee's fist. She wasn't licked yet, dammit. She might be trapped by circumstance temporarily, but she'd win in the end. She always did. It just took a little determination. It took sticking to her goals until they were reached. The only difference was—much as she hated to admit it—she couldn't do it alone this time.

But she didn't have to sit around and take his guff, either. She'd been crammed into that stupid car for too long with that self-righteous bully. Petulantly, she watched as Dex spoke to the bartender, who shook his head and spread his hands.

Water for the car, she remembered. He probably doesn't have anything to carry it in.

But she knew who would, and how she could kill two birds with one carefully placed stone.

She shifted in her seat to address the Marine who still hovered over her, halfheartedly searching for an empty seat. "Excuse me . . ." Silently she thanked the military for name ribbons. With their uniformly shaven heads, they all looked alike to her. "Stark, is it?"

Quickly, he slid into the chair close beside her. "Yes, ma'am."

She pasted a smile on her face and retreated an inch. One word from her, and she'd have a slave for life, but that's not what she had in mind. "Stark, I have a problem. My car overheated about two miles back, and I don't think Danny has any jugs for my friend to carry water." Ruthlessly, she'd assigned him the job. She was hungry. "I don't suppose you could loan him something out of your trucks."

"I can do one better, ma'am." He leaped to his feet. "The lady needs help," he told his buddies, then called to another table. "Hey, Kramer, Wochowski, gimme a hand!" They started out and gave her a disarming grin. "Don't worry, ma'am. We'll have you fixed up in no time."

Since she had the suspicion they could carry Sheila back on their shoulders if they had to, she could honestly say, "You have my complete confidence, Lance Corporal."

"I'll be pleased if you'd allow me the honor of buying you a drink, ma'am, when we get back."

She nodded. "You got it."

Dex threw a puzzled look her way as he followed Kramer. Moments later, she heard the roar of a truck's engine. She ordered a cold beer and a mountain of ribs. When they arrived, she drank deeply, bit into the spicy ambrosia, and settled back with a moan of pure pleasure as her blood sugar took a power climb. Everything was all right with the world again. She had her favorite combination for lunch, she'd rid herself of the tyrant, the car would be fixed within the hour, they'd find Jane before the bank closed, and she'd be cleared forever.

"Hey, lady." The voice rumbled like thunder.

Startled mid-bite, she glanced up to find a giant staring down at her, the same one who'd smashed his face into the table. If he had done any damage to himself, she couldn't tell. From the looks of him, more than mere wood littered his past.

She glanced around, saw only three glassy-eyed soldiers, and realized her petition for Dex had nearly emptied the bar. Apprehension shivered through her, but she'd grown up with men like him. She knew how to handle them. She gave him her best Hammer smile. "What do you want, Marine?"

He wasn't impressed. Reaching out with a hand the size of a ham, his beer-soaked breath wafting over her, he growled the four most fearsome words she'd ever heard.

"C'mon, honey. Let's dance."

Dex centered his vision on the road ahead as he left the truck in a cloud of dust. He was obliged for the speed with which the Marines had cooled Sheila's radiator, but he fumed over Beth's latest stunt. After a hellish twenty-four hours, when he'd barely kept a grip on his temper, he'd almost been grateful for her "help" until he realized it was her way of getting rid of him. She'd obviously thought herself safe in that bar.

Unfortunately, he knew better. He'd seen the gleam in their eyes. If he hadn't let his anger overcome his common sense, he wouldn't be rushing back now. Why hadn't he listened to his instincts and stayed?

Skidding into the lot, he pocketed his keys and rushed through the barroom doors. Inside, the scene that had haunted him turned into reality.

Beth stood defiantly before the mountain of human flesh who gripped her arm with an answering leer. "Let me go, or I'll dust the floor with you," she said with a snarl. "Dance with yourself, you cretin!"

Dex stalked forward. With a feral smile, he jabbed his thumb into a certain point on the Marine's wrist. The sausagelike fingers dropped away. "The lady said no," he told his startled opponent.

"I thought you weren't psychic," Beth whispered, rubbing her abused arm as she glared at the villain.

His gaze never wavered from his adversary. "I left you with a bunch of jackals," he told her. "It didn't take telepathy to figure it out. Now get under the table."

She put her hands on her hips. "This is the nineties, Dex. Women don't crawl meekly under furniture these days."

Before he could counter, the other man smiled, his teeth gleaming. "I'll show you jackal," he muttered, and swung.

Poised for such a move, Dex dodged. The momentum carried the Marine around one hundred and eighty degrees, where he hesitated, baffled to find his target gone. "A little slow on the uptake, isn't he?" Dex commented.

"He's drunk," Beth said.

The Marine spun and heaved his meaty fist again. Dex eluded the blow again, stepping neatly out of the way, watching calmly as the man staggered against a table. "I think you're right," he told her.

"Will wonders never cease," she said in amazement.

He grinned at Beth over his shoulder. "Miracles do happen."

She tossed her hair. "You didn't have to ride to my rescue, you know. My father was a sergeant major in the Corps. I could have—" Her eyes widened. "Dex!"

He ducked instinctively, then planted his stiffened palm beneath the Marine's chin in a sharp upward thrust designed to disable. The soldier's head snapped back and he reeled, his expression bewildered as he prepared for another volley. Then, like a baby in his mother's arms, he slowly closed his eyes and crumpled to the floor, landing with a thud that shook the rafters. After a moment of stunned silence, a rumbling snore reverberated around the room.

She stared down at the fallen villain. "Nice shot. Karate?"

"Nope." He stood beside her. "Three older brothers."

"Oh."

The bar suddenly was filled with uniformed men again as the rest of the Marines returned. With murmured apologies and respectful glances at Dex, they dragged their unconscious compatriot away and propped him against the wall. The owner hurried over to reassure himself that there was no damage, and railed at the troops.

Beth sighed and turned to Dex. "So, are we ready to go?"

He gaped at her as she strode off. "That's it? I save your virtue, and you can't even say 'thank you'?"

She spun on him. "For what? For a rescue I didn't need? For a virtue it's no business of yours to protect?"

"It became my business the minute you stepped into my car," he told her steadily. "Don't you realize the kind of trouble you were in?"

She huffed. "Nothing would have happened if you hadn't stormed in here. I could handle him!"

"Yeah, I saw how you handled him. In another minute you'd have been flat on your back."

For a moment, panic trembled behind the fury in her eyes. "Thanks," she muttered. "Now can we go?"

He couldn't admit that disappointment almost

overwhelmed his anger. Dammit, he thought that maybe, just this once, she'd drop that cast-iron facade. But he was wrong. "I haven't eaten yet," he said. "I'm hungry."

"Take mine." She flopped into her chair and shoved the remains of her lunch at him. "I lost my appetite."

Elizabeth sat fuming as he picked at each morsel, taking his time as he ate. He was doing it to irritate her, she knew, but dammit, why had he suddenly turned macho on her? She'd been in complete control, and he had to swagger in like some movie hero and turn it into a fiasco!

Then she frowned as she noticed the dark smudges rimming his gray eyes, the hands that were as stained and chapped as hers. He firmed his lower lip as he finished the last of his meal, and she saw that it had split open from the desert heat. He wasn't trying to goad her—she'd hurt his feelings.

Her heart thudded painfully against her chest. He'd been right there beside her the entire trip, she realized suddenly, and she'd treated him like vermin. He'd been the one who'd fixed every problem, not her. It was *his* back that had strained with the flat tire, *his* mechanical expertise that had diagnosed Sheila's engine trouble. And his quick reflexes that had saved her, dammit. All she'd done was hold a flashlight, stand on a temperamental lug wrench, bluster her way into a dangerous situation . . . and get in his way.

None of this was his fault, she thought, her head spinning. She was the one who'd never taken the time to know her coworkers for any other reason than her own corporate gain. She was the one who'd taped her password to the inside of her desk drawer. She was the idiot who'd made enemies, not friends. As usual, she'd set her sights on a target and plowed over the course she'd set, mowing down anything or anyone in her way—blaming the one person who believed in her, the only person who'd really tried to help her.

Confusion, shame, and something she couldn't identify swirled through her as she reached into her pocket for the small tube she'd transferred from her useless purse. Tears stinging her eyes, she squeezed the salve on her finger, leaned over the table, and reached for his parched lip.

He snatched her wrist before she'd even moved into his field of vision. Now she knew the basis of those amazing reflexes, and it humbled her to think of all the horrible things she'd mentally called him. "You're bleeding," she whispered.

Suspicion creased his brow as he used his free hand to touch the spot and check her statement. Elizabeth didn't blame him—the way she'd been acting, he probably thought she was going to rip his face off. "Dry air," she said.

"I'm fine," he told her, but he didn't release her.

It was a standoff. Warmth rushed to various parts of her body. She couldn't pull her gaze from his, and she found she didn't want to pull her hand away. She worked the words past a suddenly tight throat. "Let me help you."

"I've heard that before," he muttered.

Hot blood rushed to her cheeks. Sure he'd heard it—he'd said it. Many times. But she hadn't listened.

She felt yet another wall give way inside. He deserved more than her antagonism. He deserved

a bit of her trust. "John Stein loves old movies,"
she told him in a rush.

"What?" His gaze sharpened.

"It's probably nothing, just useless information.
But—" Drawing a deep breath, she dove right in.
"When you asked if I remembered anything else
about the others . . . well, John loves movies."
She saw his expression soften. "He—he has a
collection of memorabilia. Didn't you ever notice
that lamp on his desk? It's a stage light, straight
off the set of *An American in Paris.*"

"So that's what that was."

She nodded. "An agent brought it in one day,
and we talked about Selznick and Huston and Billy
Wilder." Elizabeth gulped as Dex's thumb began to
trace a slow circle on her captive wrist. "I couldn't
tell you because—" He drew her hand toward him.
Her pulse shot into overdrive. Her voice dropped
an octave. "Because then you'd know my secret."

"You collect it too?" he murmured, his thumb
moving to her palm.

"No, I—I can't afford to." The mesmerizing sleepy
gray eyes and the sensual rhythm stroking her
skin compelled her to tell the whole truth, difficult
as it was. "I love *watching* them," she whispered.
"And not only the comedies." She glanced away for
the final blow. "My favorite Saturday nights are
spent with a stack of videos, a bowl of popcorn in
one hand and a box of Kleenex in the other."

"*Dark Victory?*" he asked with a crooked smile.
"*Casablanca? Brian's Song?*"

Her mouth trembled and she nodded. "*Camille,
West Side Story,* even *Old Yeller.* You name it, I've
seen it a hundred times."

"Through your tears."

She tugged at her hand, but he wouldn't release her. "Now you know my deep, dark secret. I'm a sucker for an unhappy ending. A grown woman bawling her eyes out over a movie. Pretty silly, huh?"

"No, Beth. Not silly at all. And there's no such thing as useless information. Sometimes we simply don't see the significance." Gently he folded her fingers into her palm and pulled a single digit toward his mouth. "This time it was most illuminating."

Startled by his action—and the fact that the name didn't seem as insulting as it had before—she resisted. "What are you doing?"

"Finishing what you started," he murmured, and touched the salve to his lip.

Elizabeth felt the graze of his rough skin against her soft. Her blood rushed through her, swirling into fiery whirlpools at dozens of strategic locations. Every nerve in her body saluted and stood at attention.

All from a single caress.

Gasping, she jerked her hand from his. "Dex, I—" She cut herself off, battling her conflicting emotions.

"What?"

He was focused completely on her, as if he were plumbing the depths of her soul. "I—" She felt herself drowning in him, yearning to touch him, to be the kind of woman he wanted . . . the kind of woman she might have been if she'd never found out that the meek only inherited the earth when the bullies allowed it.

Rubbing her tingling palms over her jeans, she

tore her gaze away, avoiding his astute scrutiny. "Nothing. Are you ready to go?" Without waiting for an answer, she slid out of the seat and headed toward the door.

"I'll meet you outside," he called, confusion evident in his voice.

She waved her hand and shoved through the door into the heat, drinking in the clear air, untainted by smog. Once there, she sagged against the splintered wall, swallowing a tight lump of longing. It would be the biggest mistake of her life to give in to the strange urgings of her body.

And what could she tell him? That the brush of his lip on her finger had been the most erotic sensation she'd ever experienced? That he was the most sensual man she'd ever known? That she wanted to touch him all over, feel his hands on her until she begged for release? She refused to sound like a naive thirties heroine.

Besides, she thought, hugging herself against a sudden chill, he wasn't her type at all. He had no ambition, no drive to succeed, and he was over-protective and old-fashioned to boot.

One more day, she told herself firmly. In twenty-four hours the quest for her elusive assistant would be over, and they would be free of each other forever.

Why did the thought cause her so much hurt?

When she saw him exit the bar, she strode with him toward the car. "Do you think the budget can stretch to a motel?" Her heartbeat quickened. She told it to shut up. "Two rooms, of course."

He reached out to guide her past a post. "We'll

manage for one night." He turned her to him. "But we can still go back to San Francisco."

His face loomed above her, his warm gray eyes as overwhelming and intense as the starlit sky. Silver moonlight outlined the features she knew were imprinted on her memory forever. She found herself holding her breath. "Is that what your instincts tell you?"

He gave her a wry smile and leaned down. "My instincts are in chaos lately," he whispered, and covered her mouth with his.

The kiss was as soft as the desert night, a butterfly brush of skin. And when he drew back, all too soon for her thirsty senses, she licked her suddenly dry lips, tasting the minty salve, and stared up at him in confusion. "Why did you do that?"

"Beth—"

Panic washed over her. She backed away from him, shaking her head. "Don't call me that," she said in a raspy voice. "I'm not a 'Beth,' and I'm not food for your web, Spiderman. My name is Elizabeth, and I *earned* the only nickname I have. Fairly—no corporate games, and no insider trading. I might have gotten my job by connections, but by God, I've more than proved myself!" She jerked open her door, baffled to find herself on the verge of tears. "Let's get out of here."

"You're a very determined woman."

"Damned straight." She stared through the windshield, realizing she needed to say more. She didn't want her sharp tongue to ruin their tenuous truce. "Dex?" she said, her voice quavering.

He had reached for the key, but he paused. "What?"

"Thanks for the rescue."

After an eternal hesitation, he switched on the engine. "You're welcome, *partner*."

She bit her lip to still a trembling smile. "Let's go back to 'Beth,'" she muttered.

Four

For a regional headquarters of a major bank, the single-story building was hardly imposing, Elizabeth thought as she mopped her forehead. Its peachy, pseudo-Spanish facade fit perfectly into the rest of the Tempe shopping district, its huge windows allowing a glimpse of the beehive of activity inside. Her vantage point in the coffee shop across the street gave her a perfect view. She could see every move Dex made.

Which, at this point, had been a total of one.

She nibbled a cracker, sitting straighter as he finally slipped through the door. A quick glance at her watch told her he'd stood outside for a full three minutes tying nonexistent shoelaces as he studied the crowd through the windows. She clenched her fists when, in typical fashion, he paused just inside and surveyed the office, unobtrusively scrutinizing each employee, deciding on the perfect target.

"Get on with it," she whispered, but he simply stood.

Her stomach heaved. Dammit, all he had to do was find out what had happened to Jane, or, barring that, get into her office and discover her home address. Admittedly the latter was a seemingly impossible task, knowing Jane's paranoid need for concealment, but why did Dex always make things so complicated? Didn't he realize how suspicious his actions might seem, especially on payday, when the bank held thousands of extra dollars in cash? Since they were both dressed in the same clothes they'd worn for the last two days—albeit washed and dried in the motel rooms' respective sinks—he hardly looked like a respectable customer. If he kept standing there like a lawn jockey, all he was going to do was draw attention to himself!

Unable to torture herself another moment, she turned away and sipped her cooling tea. Dex's innate, instinctive caution was going to kill her, she decided. After their blessedly uneventful drive into Phoenix the night before, they'd spoken of this venture, but the words had hardly been calculated to ease her peace of mind.

"Does Jane frighten easily?" he'd asked her after he'd registered them at the decent but inexpensive motel. At her disgusted nod, he'd shaken his head. "Your story was picked up by the media, remember. Either she'll call your office with the facts you need, or she'll panic and run. We'll see in the morning." He'd hesitated, then showed a brief flash of anxiety. "Beth, it would be so much easier if we went back. I could find the missing link in my research, and I could protect you from—"

"No! I don't care how I get it, but I need to know who was using my terminal. I need Jane." And she

needed to know she was in command, or everything would fall apart again.

Her private battle had cost her. Though she'd
been exhausted, her night had been restless
snatches of sleep, haunted by the kiss they'd
shared, the emotions she'd bottled up for so long.
She had awakened with the sun, unable to figure
out which had frightened her more.

They'd found the news item at breakfast, on
page six, saying only that Elizabeth was wanted
for questioning. But Elizabeth knew Jane read
every paper cover-to-cover. A quick, nasal call to
her own executive office revealed that no one had
cleared her. Another found that Jane still hadn't
returned to her branch.

Elizabeth checked Dex's position in the bank—
unchanged—and pressed a fist to her burning
stomach. This whole catastrophe had activated a
childhood ailment—the nervous stomach that had
given her father such exasperation. If Dex didn't
hurry, she was going to need a hospital. It chafed
that she couldn't go in herself, but Dex had
pointed out that working banks had video cameras. Though this was a regional office, they still
had all the services of a regular branch—one of her
own bright ideas to cut the budget, she thought in
disgust. Even if no one recognized her right away,
they'd have a visual record of her visit. She
couldn't afford to broadcast her whereabouts, not
yet. Not until they'd found Jane and the proof she
needed.

"Señorita?"

Elizabeth jumped and snapped her attention to
the pretty waitress who stood beside her with a
question in her eye and a carafe of hot water in

her hand. Swallowing convulsively, Elizabeth pasted a smile on her lips and pushed the empty cup toward her.

The waitress paused in the act of pouring. "Are you sure you want more of the same?" she asked. "You look a little jumpy. We have herbal, you know."

Elizabeth declined her offer with more vehemence than grace, and the girl shrugged and wandered off. Elizabeth dunked the new bag in the water and turned back to the window.

He wasn't there.

Panic skittered along her spine. She craned her neck and half-stood before she saw his rangy figure leaning over a desk to the right, facing an attractive brunette. Dizzy with relief, she returned to her seat, wishing she could hear the conversation.

He tossed his head back in laughter, nodded, and took the woman's hand, obviously commiserating with her. Elizabeth turned away as something surged in her veins. Adrenaline, she told herself firmly. Of course that's all it was, excitement that he'd obviously made a successful first move. She gritted her teeth and sipped her tea.

The bag bumped her lip. Irritably, she tossed it to the table, where it landed with a splat, then she spooned in sugar. Stirring absently, she returned her gaze to Dex and the secretary, who were now bent together in earnest conversation. She raised the cup, freezing halfway as Dex touched the woman's shoulder—*caressed* it—then nodded. They both headed into an office, which luckily fronted the street, though vertical blinds closed off part of it. Anxiously, she waited for them to appear, to go to the desk she could see clearly on the left.

Any second now, she thought, they'd move into sight. Any second now. She leaned to the edge of her seat. Any second now.

Elizabeth dropped her cup with a clatter when the seconds stretched into a minute, then into two. Not that she cared how he obtained the information, of course, but she hadn't thought he'd demean himself by . . . she hadn't figured he'd stoop to such a level as to . . . that he'd actually . . .

Infuriated that she couldn't even finish the thought, Elizabeth groped for the spoon and the sugar, her gaze never wavering from the office across the street. "Come on," she whispered. "What's going on?"

Suddenly, the brunette walked into view, looking the same as she had before. Elizabeth sagged in relief—because she could now see what was happening, she told herself hastily.

The woman gestured to a telephone and nodded at some unheard question. She clasped her hands together, nodded again, and left the office, then reappeared a moment later at her own desk.

While she answered a customer's question and pulled a steno pad out of her drawer, Dex paced through the office, then slid open the file cabinet.

"No, dammit," Elizabeth whispered, disgusted. "She wouldn't leave an address on other people's files!"

Apparently he agreed. He shut the doors and put his hands on his lean hips, striding the length of the room. He paused to examine the desk top, hesitated, then shuffled through a pile of papers and plucked one up.

Elizabeth glanced to the other side. She tensed, her heart pounding a staccato rhythm. The secretary had already headed back, and Dex was grinning over his find as if he had all the time in the world! Silently she screamed a warning.

He leaned to detach it from something, then stuffed the paper down the front of his pants at the same moment the woman pushed through the door.

Elizabeth nearly fainted.

Closing her eyes, she wavered in her chair, refusing to watch the rest of the show. He had information and he was safe, that's all that mattered. She clasped her trembling hands together around her warm cup, confused to realize she didn't know which was more important to her.

She still hadn't decided when she glanced up to find him bounding toward the cafe, a grin lighting his rugged features. Her spirits soared, but she ignored the obvious reason, though she couldn't help but smile at his attitude. Whether he wanted to admit it or not, he loved this cloak-and-dagger game. She fought down the urge to meet the stubborn daredevil in the street and throw her arms around his neck, deciding that he didn't deserve it. Hell, he'd had all the fun! She'd had to sit listening to her nerves eat through her stomach lining! This was *her* arrest, not his, and he never let her do anything!

When he at last stood beside her, she'd worked herself into a boiling state of righteous indignation. "What in the name of all that's holy were you doing over there?" she asked. "You stared through that window so long, I thought you'd burn a hole in it!"

"I couldn't simply waltz in." He seated himself quickly, keeping the building in full view. "I had to find the blind spots in the video scans."

Deflated as usual by his calm logic, Elizabeth ran impatient fingers through her hair. At the rate she was going, she'd be bald by the time they found Jane. "All right, Sherlock," she said in a more reasonable tone, "what did you discover?"

"Jane's not there." He picked up her cup.

"I think we'd already established that," she said with infinite patience.

"Yes, but she hasn't been there since yesterday." He sipped. "She was—" He cut himself off with a shudder and dropped the cup to the saucer. After peering into the nearly empty sugar bowl, he raised his brows at her. "Like a little tea with your syrup?"

Elizabeth felt a blush creep into her cheeks. She'd been so jealous—no, anxious!—she must have spooned half a cane field into her cup. "What else did you find out?" she asked. "I saw you take something from Jane's desk."

"Oh, that," he said with a smug smile, letting his gaze wander to the street. "I think—" His grin faded abruptly, and he stood. "Have you paid the bill?" he asked in a low, urgent tone.

"Not yet."

He swore and tossed a couple of dollars to the table, grabbing her arm. "Let's get out of here."

Puzzled, Elizabeth followed his gaze. Two patrol cars sat parked at the curb in front of the bank. "Dex, what did you do?"

He hurried her out the door. "You needed something with her home address on it."

"And you got it?" She ran to keep up with his long-legged stride, astonished at his accomplishment. Then terror shivered through her. Good Lord, he must have stolen some ultrasecret document or a million-dollar lottery ticket to be in this much of a hurry. "Dex, what did you take?"

"It was sitting on Jane's desk, big as life." He hesitated, as if to tell her more, then shook his head and stuffed her into Sheila. "Also I, uh, sort of let her secretary think I was with the police." He slid across the hood to dive into the driver's seat, then started the engine and slammed into gear.

Elizabeth gasped as the tires squealed in protest. "You impersonated a police officer?"

"She did all the assuming. I just didn't correct her." At the first stoplight, he glanced behind them. Then, one hand on the steering wheel, he stretched up and reached into his jeans. He frowned. "It couldn't have fallen out," he muttered.

A decidedly bawdy comment rose to mind, but Elizabeth tensed at the thought of lost evidence. To be so close . . .

Dex glowered, groped to one side, then sighed in relief. Slowly he pulled a white envelope from his waistband.

"What is it?" she asked breathlessly.

He shrugged. "Nothing much." He fanned it in the air and grinned. "Just her paycheck stub."

Elizabeth fought the laughter for all of two seconds. But she couldn't help herself. She threw back her head and laughed as she hadn't in years. "Dexter Wolffe," she cried, wiping the tears from her cheeks, "you are a first-class, dyed-in-the-wool genius!"

He nodded modestly. "I know."

Elizabeth glanced up from her map, stuck a piece of beef jerky into her mouth—both of which they'd purchased at the first gas station they'd found—and tucked a stray wisp of hair behind her ear. "At the next big intersection, turn left."

"Left," Dex repeated with a smile. While he watched for the correct street, he kept her firmly in his peripheral vision, amazed at the change in her in the last hour. The sunlight made her hair glow like a cotton-candy halo and colored her freckled skin a warm peach. He could see her nipples hard with excitement through the thin material of her ridiculous T-shirt.

He shifted away from that line of thought. Though he'd despised her when he thought her too much like Amber, he was disturbed that the pendulum had swung the other way. He hadn't wanted to admit how worried he'd been all night. After he'd shown her the article that morning, her complexion had become pale and waxy, her blue eyes dull instead of sparkling, as they were now. She'd moved like a twitchy puppet, she'd snapped at every word he'd spoken, and she had completely lost her appetite.

Now she burned with the fire of purpose, her cheeks flushed at the prospect of finding Jane. She was so happy to be close to her goal.

His smile faded as he remembered the rest of the information he'd obtained from the secretary—the phone call Jane had received before she'd even finished her first cup of coffee, the harried look on her face when she'd left minutes later, never to return.

Every instinct he possessed told him there was no way on earth Jane was at home. Still he didn't have the heart to burst Beth's bubble. An occasional shot at her arrogance was one thing; it was for her own good. But now she had her hope back, and he couldn't take that away from her.

But he couldn't let her walk headlong into disappointment, either.

He signaled and made the correct turn, frowning as he constructed his warning. "Beth?"

"Hmm?" she murmured, her gaze firmly on the map as she measured it against the jerky.

"What if Jane's not there?"

"Jane always holed up at home when she stressed out," she said, apparently ruling out such an eventuality. She turned the paper sideways, then laid it back in her lap. "Okay, if the scale is correct, we go a mile, then left again."

Glancing at the odometer, he switched that part of his mind into automatic and decided that Elizabeth Hamner made a Missouri mule look like a Boston cream puff. "Humor me. If Jane's not there, we'll need an alternative plan of action. Obviously, you'll want to pursue her."

Elizabeth checked the passing street signs. "Obviously," she repeated absently, then nodded, ripped off a chunk of beef, and returned to her map.

"And that means finding out if she has any family to run to."

"She was an only child and her parents died her senior year in high school. No aunts, uncles, or otherwise, which is why she married that no-good bum so young." She gave Dex the summary as if she were reciting a financial report. "It's the next turn."

Sighing, Dex cleared the corner and mentally regrouped, slowing their speed as they moved into a residential neighborhood. "If she has no family, she might just take off, then. If she's run from her husband before, she probably knows how to hide effectively."

"Right."

"Right," he repeated, feeling as if he were finally getting through that stubborn skull of hers. "And we could—"

"Dex, right!" She grabbed the steering wheel. "Turn right!"

Startled, he swerved, barely avoiding an oncoming van. He glared at her innocent, wide-eyed expression. Hesitantly she popped another piece of jerky into her mouth and chewed.

He took a deep, cleansing breath and returned his attention to the road. "Don't *ever* do that again," he said ominously.

She choked and turned away, ostensibly scanning the brick houses for the correct number. He wasn't fooled into thinking she was intimidated. He'd seen her smile.

And he'd lost his opportunity to cushion the possible blow. Within moments, they found Jane's single-story home. Its white trim and pink-draped windows made it quaint rather than small. Several compact cars were parked around the neighborhood. He eased to a stop at the curb.

Elizabeth tossed her snack to the floor and flung open Sheila's door. But before she could scramble out, he caught her arm. "Beth, if she's not here—"

She frowned at his hand and shook it off, sliding out of the car and striding toward the house. "We can't determine that from the car, now can we?" she called over her shoulder. She flew up the porch and pounded on the front door.

So much for breaking it to her gently, he thought as he walked up the sidewalk. He glanced around, the only sign of life a black Sundance pulling into a driveway. He fixed his attention on Beth. She knocked again before he reached the concrete steps. "Beth—"

"Around back," she said, and scurried to the side. By the time he'd caught up with her, she was peering through a window, her hands cupped on either side of her face. "Dex, look!"

"She's here?" Disbelieving, he peered inside, too, but he could see no sign of movement. "She's gone."

"I know that, but look."

It was a bedroom, he saw that much. Then he understood what she meant—drawers stood open, clothes were scattered about and hanging off the twin lamps. The bed was made, but the pillows were gone.

"Either somebody did a really sloppy search job," she said, "or Jane left in a big hurry." She stood back. "Let's see if the rest of the house is this bad."

He gaped at her. "You never thought she'd be here, did you?"

"I'd hoped . . ." She shook her head and put her hands on her hips. "It doesn't take instincts to figure it out, Spiderman. You said Jane was at work yesterday, and you avoided telling me anything else." A smug smile pulled at her full mouth.

"Since I know you're an overprotective Neanderthal, and I know how the bad guys worked with me, I assumed Jane received a threatening letter or phone call. It would have had to reach her at the office, and it was probably aimed at her kids." Her smile faded. "This creep really knows our weaknesses."

For a moment, she wavered, as if faint. He took a step forward, but she squared her shoulders, spun on her heel, and headed toward another window. Her flip-flops crunched over the yellowed grass as they left the sun for the shady side of the house. "Jane took it to heart," she continued, "just the same as I did, and she lit out like the plague. Since her secretary thought you were a cop, I'd guess they were there yesterday, but she'd gone home early and missed their questions." She glanced over her shoulder. "How am I doing?"

"I'm impressed," he said, and he was. Once again, he'd underestimated her. And this facet of her competitive personality intrigued him all the more.

She peeked through the glass, and cocked her head when a stray breeze brought the fleeting sound of a distant siren. After a moment, she shook herself and indicated the window with a trembling hand. "Girl's room, same condition." She grinned at him. "Shall I dazzle you some more?"

Dex noticed she had paled again beneath her sunburn, and her legs wobbled when she walked. He frowned. "Let's get back to the car."

She opened her mouth to protest, then strode back the way they'd come. "Can't handle the competition, huh?" she teased in passing.

Any hopes that she was heading toward Sheila were dashed when she paused beneath another window, which was higher than the others. She glanced around for something to stand on, saw nothing, and raised her brows in inquiry. Knowing she wouldn't leave until she'd satisfied her curiosity, he cupped his hands. She kicked off her thongs and gave him her foot. He hefted her as if she weighed nothing, then swallowed hard as he faced her backside. With anyone else it would have been embarrassing; with Elizabeth it was downright erotic.

He pinched his eyes shut when she stretched to the top of the sill for balance, the movement pulling her dark T-shirt to her waist. An inch of skin showed above her pants, revealing a tiny, heart-shaped mole on the left. All he'd have to do was tilt his head and nibble.

Sure. Then she'd scream and turn into the Wicked Sergeant Major of the West. He couldn't afford to invoke her demons with an impulsive pass. Or should he? he wondered, frowning.

After another quick survey, Elizabeth reported that it was indeed the bathroom, and that the medicine cabinet had been cleared.

"I can see through to the living room," she told him. "It's immaculate."

"You didn't really think it would be searched, did you?" he asked as she hopped down. "The information she has is in her head, not on paper."

"I know." She leaned back against the wall, smiling up at him as if she'd found the Holy Grail. "Don't you understand what this means?"

Dex frowned, trying to pull together the clues already in his mind. He *knew* the answer, dammit, but his only coherent thoughts revolved around the feel of her arch in his palm and the way she took the stretch right out of those jeans! He wished he could block out the sight of her breasts pushing into that ridiculously large T-shirt, or the unintentionally inviting curve of her body pressed against the house, or the bright hue of her cheeks, or the sparkle of her eyes like a windblown lake in spring. But he couldn't find the strength to close his lids again.

"Dex? Don't you see?"

Too much, he thought to himself. "Sure," he said, and cleared his dry throat when the word rasped out. With the effort of a drowning man, he reined in his growing desire and gathered his scattered wits. Logic, he told himself firmly, at least her version of it. All he needed was to pull her erratic data together, think like Elizabeth and . . .

He grinned. "If Jane knew nothing, she wouldn't need to run. Therefore—"

"Jane can clear me," she whispered triumphantly, then reached out to touch his chest. "Thank you, Dex. You believe me now, don't you?"

He nodded, feeling his heart pound against her fingertips. "We're still a long way from the end of this," he warned. "We'll have to find her all over again."

"I know. But you won't try and talk me out of this anymore, will you?"

"No, Beth. I won't." His breath caught as her smile faded and her palm pressed closer. A rogue breeze brought the scent of some sweet desert flower, then lifted her hair in a pagan dance. He bent his head, feeling the silky stroke of her hair against his cheek as his mouth met her parted lips.

At the soft touch of his lips on hers, her eyelids began to drop, lanquid in her surrender. His arousal filled him with slow heat. He drew back to find her as lost in the kiss as he, and he bent toward her once more.

The rising wail seemed to echo his growing passion with such accuracy that he didn't realize its implications at first. But the quiet part of his mind, always on alert, finally shoved into the peaceful haven they'd created between them.

He jerked his head up. She blinked dazed eyes. Then she heard it, too, and paled to a deathly gray.

"Ohmygod," she whispered. "The police!"

Five

Dex hushed her and listened, praying the sound would fade. When it grew louder instead, he swore and turned, but Elizabeth's frozen figure halted his flight.

He took her shoulders and peered into her chalky face. "Dammit, don't lose it on me now, Beth."

For a split second he thought her completely paralyzed. Her slender frame trembled beneath his palms, her breath came in shallow gasps. He shook her firmly. "Hammer, we have to go."

To his relief, she focused on him and nodded. Without a word, she slipped from him and began to run. He followed, nearly toppling them both when she spun in her tracks. "My shoes," she explained in a frighteningly reasonable tone.

"We'll get another pair!"

She raced past him. "We can't afford it."

Before his impatience made him swear again, she was back, glancing upward as the siren filled the air. Like Chicken Little waiting for the sky to fall, he thought, his heart catching. He bundled her into his arms and guided her to the street.

Moments later they dove into Sheila and eased away from the curb at the sedate speed limit. Since the police hadn't arrived, they didn't want to draw any more attention to themselves than necessary. Grimly, Dex concentrated on the road before him, debating their next course of action. "If someone saw us and thought we were trying to break in, the police might have a description of the car. We'd have to rent another one to continue the search."

Elizabeth huddled in her seat, clutching her stomach. "But—but if it's about Jane's disappearance, we're safe, right?"

That was the sixty-four-thousand-dollar question. "Maybe," he said.

At the corner ahead he had a choice of a side street or a dead end. He chose the latter.

"What are you doing?" Her voice had an hysterical edge. "Dex, we have to get out of here!"

"We're all right."

She reached for the steering wheel. "No, no, no!"

He blocked her. "I told you not to do that again."

She hesitated. Then reason—and fury—returned. She flounced back. "You're penning us in, Dex. We're trapped."

One corner of his mouth lifted. "Not necessarily." He swung around in the cul-de-sac, pulled over, leaving the engine running, then rolled down the window. The siren cut off abruptly. He peered at the dashboard clock.

Elizabeth groaned. "Lord, please let him know what he's doing."

"Trust me," he murmured.

"Stop saying that," she snapped out. She'd stopped shaking, but though her eyes burned with rage, her color hadn't returned.

He took her clammy hand, intending to reassure her, even if he had to Super-Glue them together. She surprised him by lacing her fingers in his and squeezing with bone-crunching force.

She started when she realized what she'd done, and tried to pull away. He tightened his grip, surprised to find that he was drawing strength from her touch too. "You go ahead and hold on," he told her gently.

"Just because I'm a little scared doesn't mean I've given up."

"I know."

"And that kiss was . . ." She trailed off, confusion shadowing her face.

He wondered why she didn't simply blast him and get it over with. "What about the kiss?"

She glanced away with a shrug. "Do you realize you have no nervous habits?"

"What?" he asked, startled by her statement.

"Most people would twist that ring of yours or drum their fingers or something."

"I don't get nervous."

"Oh." Her grip tightened, her brave tone quavered. "If you're wrong about the police . . ."

"I'm never wrong."

She gave an unladylike snort. He grinned, relieved with this further evidence that she was nearly back to normal. Her knees were still drawn up, her skin ashen, but her fighting spirit lived on.

Funny, it didn't irritate him at all anymore. He could understand apprehension, even fear, but this crippling panic just didn't fit the woman he was beginning to know so well. It pleased him to have his sparring partner return. He wondered if he'd always felt this way.

He shook off the stray thought and checked the clock. "Ready?" he asked.

After a convulsive swallow and an equally jerky squeeze of his fingers, she pulled her hand back and croaked, "Ready."

Holding Sheila in firm check, he retraced their route. At the intersection, the hairs on the nape of his neck ruffled, his senses snapped into full alert, and he slowed. But a glance around showed only an older woman tending her petunias and three cars parked near the corner—a Sundance, an Accord, and a Mustang convertible. Since he saw no rational reason for alarm, he chalked up his reaction to the approaching confrontation.

As they passed Jane's house, Elizabeth gasped when she spied the patrol car. "Hurry," she said.

"Not yet," he shot back, seeing what she obviously did not. The uniformed officers were standing on the sidewalk, not prowling the yard. They appeared bored, not anxious; one had opened his notebook to study it. As Sheila purred by, the other officer glanced up, did a double take, and elbowed his partner.

Elizabeth's fingernails ripped into Sheila's upholstery.

The second cop smiled and eased back his hat. The first whistled and flapped his open hand before himself, universal signs of male appreciation.

And Dex had seen both men before—in front of the bank.

"They like Sheila," he told her with a grin.

"They would," she muttered out of habit, not even flinching when the car surged, then resumed its normal speed. She twisted her neck around, keeping the officers in sight until a bend in the road obscured them. When she was certain no *French Connection* chase scene was imminent, she settled back into her seat and wiped her forehead. "I'd feel a lot better if I knew they weren't following us."

"They're not." But as he pulled onto the main road, Dex realized that something, some small detail overlooked by his conscious mind, still niggled at him. Instinctively, he headed away from their motel. "Let's go sightseeing," he said brightly.

Dex glanced in his rearview mirror periodically as they wandered the wide, palm-lined streets of Tempe. Nothing confirmed his vague apprehension, but he couldn't relax his guard. Not where Beth's safety was concerned.

Frowning, he studied her from the corner of his eye. She hadn't said a word in the last hour—other than a brief comment that the university's music building looked like a giant chocolate wedding cake—and it was beginning to worry him. She simply sat, rubbing her stomach.

By the time they'd left a colorfully renovated shopping district behind, he'd almost dismissed his anxiety. But not quite. Dex followed the curve of the road around a butte, watching for a busy restaurant. What they needed now was food and a crowd, he decided—one to appease her obvious hunger, the other to pacify his instinct for concealment—but they traveled a straight stretch, barren of amenities. When he spied the sign for Papago Park, and nothing but warehouses ahead of them, he turned in.

A slow sweep of the area revealed no possibility for camouflage in the picnic section. The park, nestled in the middle of an arid desert, consisted of concrete tables, rocks in every earth tone imaginable, and heavy, freestanding awnings that protected picnickers from the harsh sun while allowing a breeze. Though the park was starkly beautiful, Dex realized that glossy-white Sheila would stand out there like a neon sign.

Except at the zoo. Even at this hour of the morning—or perhaps because of it—its parking lot provided ample cover. Thinking they could at least pick up a hot dog, he checked his mirror again, then turned in and squeezed Sheila between a huge recreational vehicle and a school bus.

"A sudden urge to feed the elephants?" she murmured as he killed the engine.

He smiled at the reluctant humor in her voice. "Why not?" he countered. "We deserve a break."

"Can we afford it?"

He opened his door, letting in a whoosh of warm, dry air. "Can we afford not to?" he muttered, out of the range of her hearing.

They edged into a group of elderly matrons who strolled at a very leisurely pace through the lot, then followed them over the arched wooden bridge toward the entrance. Several stopped to feed the ducks who swam in the moat beneath them. After a quick glance over his shoulder, Dex took Beth's arm and left them behind, heading toward the group of schoolchildren who pushed through the turnstiles. They pretended to herd them in, smiled at the attendant who waved them on, and then, once in the open entrance, successfully dodged the small bodies and strode toward a cluster of picnic tables beside the rest rooms.

"Hey!" she cried after tripping over a backpack. "Slow down!"

No one had pursued them inside, he decided after a quick visual sweep of the area. And he reluctantly admitted he had no rational reason to believe they would. Dex checked his pace, puzzled by his earlier anxiety.

"Why were you running?" she asked. "Police?"

Kicking himself for alarming her, Dex shook his head. "I'm starving, that's all. Aren't you?"

She relaxed, but swallowed convulsively. "Just thirsty."

"Great." He settled her beneath a striped umbrella. "Soda? Coffee? Lemonade?"

"Anything with ice," she murmured, and lowered her face to her hands. "Take your time. I'm not going anywhere."

Dex hesitated. "Are you sick?"

"I'm never sick," she told him in no uncertain terms.

He frowned, wondering what was wrong, then shrugged and headed toward the concession stand. She was exhausted and tense, that's all. The last few days would have tested a statue's endurance. Anyone else would be hysterical by now, and he realized his predominant emotion was admiration.

As the counter girl heaped chili and cheese on his hot dogs, Dex found his thoughts straying to the kiss he and Beth had shared against Jane's house, and respect turned to arousal. The intensity didn't surprise him anymore. Three days ago he'd thought her a human piranha, but this experience had changed the way he saw her.

As he turned he paused, his hands full, and watched her. She sat turned around on the bench, staring at a pair of peacocks who strutted between the tables, pecking for crumbs. Silver-blonde hair tumbled to her hunched shoulders; her pale, freckled face looked years younger beneath its gentle caress. With her slender torso lost in that T-shirt and her ankles primly crossed beneath her, she looked more like a schoolgirl than a ruthless executive. She wasn't the woman who'd kidnapped him in San Francisco, stomped barefoot into a storm, and stood up to a drunken Marine. That woman hadn't needed anyone.

This one did.

He returned to the table and set their lunch in the middle. "Do you want any of this?" he asked.

Slowly she turned her head to appraise his offering. "Maybe a little," she told him, then picked at his fries, pausing only to stick a straw into the plastic-lidded drink.

Dex caught a grin, but it faded, and he wondered again about her earlier reaction. Casually, he told her, "You don't have to panic every time the police are around."

She froze and shot him a guarded look. "Wouldn't you if they were after you?"

"We don't know they're after anyone."

She used a french fry to wipe up the salt in the bottom of the carton. "I'm not guilty, if that's what you were thinking."

"It never crossed my mind," he told her truthfully, then leaned forward. "Stop worrying. We're going to clear you."

"Who's worried?" She stood and walked to the oilcan trash container, dropped the fry box into it, then returned, all without once looking at him. Sitting with her back to the table, she sipped from her lemonade. "Did you know peacocks sneeze?" she asked suddenly.

Startled into a chuckle by her non sequitur, he said, "No, I didn't."

With her straw, she indicated the colorful male. "He definitely sneezed while you were gone." She shook her head. "I never thought of birds sneezing."

He unwrapped a chili dog. He knew a change of subject when he heard it. He realized he'd been diverted again, but he'd get another chance. "I guess if you think about it, anything with a nose would sneeze."

"But they have no noses, just those little slits in their beaks." She sighed and drank again. "It just doesn't seem fair that such a majestic animal should do something as plebeian and gross as sneeze. Anything that regal should have it erased from his genes." She subsided and sipped some more, gazing unfocused as the peacocks went farther afield for their meal.

Dex opened his second dog, smiling at her flawless profile as he wondered why he'd never noticed what a unique mind she had. This shark in a T-shirt might be a lot of things, but she wasn't boring.

A breeze wafted through, carrying with it the soft brays and growls—and the faint odor—of the zoo's inmates. "Want to walk?" she asked.

"Sure." Carrying the remainder of his lunch, he rose and followed.

They strolled through the rows of caged birds, avoided the crowded children's section, then headed down a vacant, arid section without saying a word. Dex barely noticed the absence of animals. He watched Beth walk as if on eggshells, occasionally rubbing her throat or stomach while she sipped from her cup or, when that was empty, stopping at each of the drinking fountains that were situated at closely spaced intervals. Intrigued by her quiet, introspective mood, he remained silent, hoping she'd eventually tell him what she was thinking.

She paused midway down the trail to smile at a cataract, placed like an oasis in the barren ground. The water cascaded over layered flagstones to a small pool; there it was pumped up and released at the top again.

Beth stepped forward to touch one of the myriad of tiny green plants growing along the fall's path. "This is so pretty," she murmured, then straightened to admire it anew. "I would love something like this in my backyard."

His mind automatically analyzed the problem. "It shouldn't be too difficult to build."

She hesitated, then shook her head sadly, indicating the surrounding parched area as she tucked a dislodged lock of hair behind her ear. "It wouldn't be the same in San Francisco," she said sadly. "Its beauty lies in the fact that it's unexpected."

A statement that perfectly described her, he thought as she wandered away. Her hips swayed gently beneath the tail of the shirt; the soft, warm breeze rippled her silky hair across her shoulders.

His heart gave a strange half-skip, then seemed to swell. Frowning, he rubbed the spot and followed her, wondering what other surprises she held in store.

When they returned to the populated area, her pace increased to a fair imitation of her usual stride. "We have to plan," she told him as they entered the predators section. She paused at the wolves and shoved back her hair. "There must be a way to find Jane. Obviously she left no clues at work, but I don't think we'll have to break into her house. She's too careful to leave anything behind."

For some reason, he was disappointed she hadn't been thinking of their kiss. "Shoot, and I wanted to try out my lock picks."

Her glance fell on a group of kids, who stared back, giggling at the slogan on her shirt. "A better place to start is the school. She wouldn't take off without her kids. One of them might have let something slip before they left."

Not a shark or even a piranha, he decided. Elizabeth Hamner was a blonde Rat Terrier. He almost missed her silence. With a sigh, he tried to analyze things. "Okay," he said, stepping alongside her, "I could trace her credit cards. Not everyone loses them on a rainy road, you know."

One corner of her mouth lifted. "Is that a dig?"

"Yes."

"At least I use them." She leaned her elbows on the rail, frowning. "You'll need a computer for that, won't you?"

"We should be able to find a place that rents. But it won't be cheap." A cost-saving idea occurred to him, bringing with it a sudden, overwhelming surge of arousal at the image it evoked. For that reason, he hesitated to voice the solution.

"And that's not all." She indicated her shirt and his sweater. "We're not exactly doing very well in the incognito department. Cable-knit is great in the fog, but not in a furnace. We need new clothes. Can we afford all this?"

"We can always find a thrift shop. But you're right. An extended search isn't feasible." Lord, why was it so difficult to tell her his idea when it appealed to him so much?

Because if he blurted it out, she'd puff up faster than a scalded cat, he thought.

"We're running short of cash," he said finally. "In another couple of days we're going to be tapped." Taking a deep breath, he dove in. "As I see it we have three choices. We could find a way to earn the funds we need—"

"Without a social security card, that would be interesting," she murmured.

"—we can go back to San Francisco and work on my end of the investigation—"

"Not an option," she interjected hotly.

"—or . . ."—he swallowed hard—"we move into the same room."

To his surprise, she didn't immediately begin throwing rocks at him. She stood gazing out at the pack of wolves who snapped and snarled over a scrap of hide; only the slight rocking motion of her body betrayed her irritation.

"I've realized a few things on this trip," she said. "I've realized that you're smarter than I thought you were."

"Thanks," he said, baffled.

"And you're intractable and single-minded."

"Uh-huh."

"And," she went on, "you don't know squat." She tensed. "I went to Yale on a scholarship, Dex. And I worked part-time to earn my keep. Being an only child of two working parents, I had no problem staying to myself—I didn't have time for much else anyway—and so I never needed anyone or anything. I do understand a budget. But I understand us too." After a moment, she nodded toward the animals. "That's us," she told him. "Inherent loners who've been forced together to survive. You put us in the same room, and we'll tear each other's heads off."

"They're not loners by nature," he heard himself say. Even more astonishing was the next tidbit of information his quirky brain remembered. "And they're one of the few species who mate for life."

She was so close, he could smell the elusive scent of her strawberry shampoo. He took her shoulders and felt her tremble beneath his touch. Without knowing what he truly intended to say, he leaned down and whispered her name.

She jerked back. "Don't even think it," she said. Her hand flew to her throat. "There must be another way."

"Not this time."

"Dammit, there has to be." She spun around and stomped past the garbage container. She swayed and reached out to clutch the drinking fountain. "We hate each other's guts! We disagree with everything the other stands for!"

Stunned, Dex blinked, realizing that her statement wasn't exactly true anymore. He didn't hate her at all. He was falling in love with her! When had that happened?

LET YOURSELF BE LOVESWEPT BY... SIX BRAND NEW LOVESWEPT ROMANCES!

Because Loveswept romances sell themselves ...we want to send you six (Yes, six!) exciting new novels to enjoy for 15 days — risk free! — without obligation to buy

Discover how these compelling stories of contemporary romances tug at your heart strings and keep you turning the pages. Meet true-to-life characters you'll fall in love with as their romances blossom. Experience their challenges and triumphs — their laughter, tears and passion.

Let yourself be Loveswept! Join our **at-home reader service!** Each month we'll send you six new Loveswept novels **before they appear in the bookstores.** Take up to **15 days to preview** current selections **risk-free! Keep only those shipments you want.** Each book is yours for only $2.25 plus postage & handling, and sales tax in N.Y. — **a savings of 50¢ per book** off the cover price.

NO OBLIGATION TO BUY — WITH THIS RISK-FREE OFFER!

YOU GET SIX ROMANCES RISK FREE...
Plus AN EXCLUSIVE TITLE FREE!

Loveswept Romances

```
AFFIX
RISK FREE
BOOKS
STAMP
HERE.
```

This FREE gift
is yours to keep.

MY "NO RISK" GUARANTEE

There's no obligation to buy and the free gift is mine to keep. I may preview each subsequent shipment for 15 days. If I don't want it, I simply return the books within 15 days and owe nothing. If I keep them, I will pay just $2.25 per book. I save $3.00 off the retail price for the 6 books (plus postage and handling, and sales tax in NY).

YES! Please send my six Loveswept novels RISK FREE along with my FREE GIFT described inside the heart! **RA123** 41228

NAME_____

ADDRESS_____APT_____

CITY_____

STATE_____ZIP_____

Before he could answer himself, she halted abruptly, clenching and unclenching her fists.

He stepped forward and glanced around for a uniform. Seeing none, he asked, "What's wrong?"

Her gaze sizzled. "If you think I'm going to jump into bed with you—"

"There are two beds in a double room."

"That's not what you had in mind!" She doubled over.

He leaped toward her, but she eluded him. "You need a doctor, don't you?"

Shaking her head, she walked forward. "I'm fine. It'll go away again. I don't need—I've never needed yours or anybody else's—" She twisted over. "Dammit, that hurts!"

Without a second thought, he swept her into his arms. "I'm taking you home," he told her, and when she didn't immediately argue, his concern turned to full-blown fear.

When he was younger, Dex's brothers had done their best to shake his self-command. They'd locked him in dark closets, they'd hidden rubber spiders in his lunch box, and once, with typical juvenile cruelty, they'd pretended their parents had died. But he'd turned the psychological tables on them. When he couldn't talk his way out of a situation, he'd first learned to fight, and then to coerce with the expertise of a master con artist.

In all the years he'd been the butt of their efforts, the only real fear he'd ever felt was when his oldest brother had pushed him out of a tree and broken his arm. Even then, at age six, Dex had instinctively immobilized the shattered limb and reassured the guilt-ridden Jamie before going to his parents.

Now, for the first time in his life, Dex panicked.

Forgetting the possibility of pursuit or observation—and against her increasingly vocal protests—Dex carried Elizabeth to the car. After racing to the motel, he carried her inside too. Once there, shaking like a willow in the wind, he set her gently on the room's double bed, unbuttoned her jeans, and pulled up her shirt.

She snatched it down. "What are you doing?"

He wrestled with her, then slid it up again and poked her right side. "Does this hurt?"

She pinched his hand, her eyes flashing. "Does *that* hurt?"

A "no," he decided in relief. He mentally crossed appendix rupture off his list. "Are you nauseous?"

"Not yet," she said, jerking the hem back down. "But you're pushing."

Wildly, he forced himself to go through all possibilities. "Are you pregnant?"

"Am I *what*?"

He ran a quivering hand through his hair. "I know a lot of corporate women plan—"

"Not this one!" She rolled to her side. "I'll wait until later, thank you. I haven't—I mean, I've been on the pill for two years. And *if* I decide to get pregnant, I'll do it the old-fashioned way!"

He wondered about her telltale slip, but didn't pursue it. "Is it time for your—you know?"

She bolted upright. "No, it's not time for my 'you know.' Good grief, what is it with men that they can't even say it?"

He ran out of possibilities, stood, and pulled out his keys. "I'm taking you to the hospital."

Before he could stop her, she plucked the keys from his fingers and threw them across the room.

She crossed her arms and glared at him. "I don't need some quack's diagnosis."

His fragile temper rose. "Then you tell me! What in the hell could be causing this?"

She smiled, a particularly nasty smile. "Gee, I don't know. Could it be the fact that I have to depend on a big strong man for every cent, like some archaic housewife? Or maybe it's Jane's vanishing act. Or the fact that I'm probably running from a bench warrant for a crime I didn't commit! Or—"

"The newspaper said you're wanted for questioning, not—"

"—it could be your patronizing attitude!" She waved her hands in the air. One landed on the lumpy pillow beside her. "Or these wonderfully *luxurious* accommodations!" She punched the cheap cushion and drilled him with her gaze. "Or the company I'm forced to keep!"

He leaned toward her, his fists firmly on either side. "It's no picnic for me either, sister!"

Her nostrils flared, and she leaped to her feet, clutching the pillow. "What in the hell is that supposed to mean?"

His intense, analyzing gaze raked her as he sank to the bed. He couldn't possibly love her! "Lord, you were born to the corporate mantle, weren't you? And it doesn't matter how you got there! First you order everything and everyone around to suit your own scenario, then you blame me when it doesn't go the way you thought it would. Or you tell yourself you hadn't really thought it in the first place." He shook his head. "You have an ulcer, don't you, and it's no wonder, Beth—you're a nervous wreck!"

"Don't call me that!" Her fingers dug into the bolster as another twinge of pain hit her stomach. "I haven't lost control!"

He picked up the other pillow and slammed it to his lap. "Bull. You're twisting yourself up in the details that you *can't* control, and that's ridiculous!"

Elizabeth flounced to the chair opposite him. "Ridiculous? How can focus be ridiculous?"

"You don't focus, you constrict!" He leaned over. "You torment over every detail as if one false step would send us into some kind of abyss!"

Elizabeth cuffed him with her pillow, astonished at her action. But she had to admit, the satisfaction of wiping that self-righteous expression from his face almost made up for it. "You'd rather jump in with both feet on nothing but a wing and a prayer, trusting some nebulous instinct. I can't work that way."

His eyes narrowed; his grip tightened on his pillow. "I'm not the one with the ulcer."

"Neither am I! It's a nervous stomach, and I've had it since I was fifteen!" In for a penny, in for a pound, she thought, and smacked him again. "And just who gave you the right to judge my methods?"

"We're partners." He emphasized the word by thwapping her with his pillow.

She stood and leveled one to the top of his head. "Wake up and smell the coffee, Dex! We're not partners! We never have been! We're two chiefs with no indians!"

"I don't want to boss you around!" He caught her on the backside. "I—I care about you!"

"You have a funny way of showing it!" She

launched herself to the bed, crouching to her knees beside him in a more strategic position. "Dammit!" she muttered as he bopped her on the head. She returned his fire with a vengeance.

"I love it when we communicate," he said.

"I won't be bullied!" she cried, refusing to give up, even when his next thump shoved her hair into her face. She spit it from her mouth and swung out. "What gives you the—ugh!—right to dictate to me?" Her next shot went wild, but she felt it connect.

"I'm not trying to—" He went down with a grunt, prone, his head in the lower corner of the rumpled blankets. "—to dictate anything! You're blowing this all out of proportion, as usual!"

"Ha!" Taking advantage of his new, vulnerable position, she straddled him and flung his pillow aside. After a last strike, she tossed hers away, too, and pinned his hands over his head, her chest heaving from the exertion. Uncaring of the shirt bunching around her waist, of the jeans gaping at her belly, she shook her hair from her eyes and grinned at her conquest. "Give."

"No way, lady."

He bucked, but she'd wrestled with the best of them and won before. Her obnoxious cousins had never gained the advantage, and Dex wouldn't now. She squeezed with her thighs, curling her feet into his, then pulled his legs apart to prevent his using them against her.

In her triumph, she didn't notice the fire in his gray eyes shift in intensity—not at first. "Say uncle and I'll let you up."

"Not on your life."

"Then we'll stay here until you admit it." She felt

movement beneath her, and realized it was more than involuntary. She gulped, suddenly realizing what part of his anatomy lay beneath her buttocks, and a numbing, paralyzing heat shot through her. "Admit it," she told him, her voice sounding more like a purr than the growl she'd meant it to be.

His body lifted beneath her, a parody of his earlier play for freedom. His hardened shaft rubbed against her; fire shot from her loins through her body. Her arms weakened, lowering her. "Admit it," she repeated, fighting for her reason against his assault. She couldn't allow his victory!

"Admit what?" he murmured hoarsely. Hot breath fanned her neck. "Admit that I want you? That I won't be able to sleep across from you when your scent fills the room, when I can see the sheen of your hair on the pillow, the glow of your skin so close I just have to lean over to caress it?" His fingers merged with hers. "Oh, yes, I'll admit that."

"No." Her mind told her to shift off him, but her traitorous body refused. How could she move when her breasts throbbed, her belly tightened with a knot of pure fire? "Admit that you're a tyrant." Her elbows began to tremble, her face drifted farther toward him. "Give up," she whispered, her lips brushing his.

His gaze darkened, caressing her like a veil along her skin, but he made no overt attempt to overpower her in any way. "No," he murmured, his breath sweet in her mouth. "You give up."

"Never." With a moan, she swept him into a kiss that whirled her senses with hurricane force. Her fingers convulsed, laced into his, gripping them as security, as her only solid hold in a universe gone crazy.

Fantasy, not reality.

She tore herself from him, confused by conflicting emotions, her body tight and wet and hot all over as his gray eyes pierced her. If she had her wallet, if she had a grip on her situation, none of this would be happening!

She thought of everything she wanted to say about his pigheaded determination to protect her from everyone but him; she felt like blasting his idiotic reliance on instinct instead of method, screaming about the defenses she'd spent years constructing that he'd somehow destroyed in three days. He could physically overpower her, and a part of her begged him to do it, to break this sensual web in which she'd found herself entangled. She needed something to draw her back from the edge of this reckless insanity.

But he didn't and she couldn't.

With a hungry groan, she dug her fingers into his hair and kissed him with the pent-up desires of a lifetime. His ardor matched hers, his tongue dueling, teasing, drawing her into a mere imitation of the intimate battle to come.

She moaned as his teeth nipped the vulnerable spot behind her neck. Wildly, she shoved his sweater up, over his head, his arms, her nails raking his skin as she retraced her path downward. Hands quivering, she fumbled with his jeans, forcing them past his hips, then farther.

Her body went up like dry kindling as he stripped her shirt from her torso and pulled her naked breasts against the rough curls on his chest. Sliding downward, she gasped, her sensitized nipples tugging at the deepest part of her womanhood.

Savagely, she peeled her jeans off and tossed them to the floor. Whatever the uncertain future held, she needed this, she needed him, now. This man excited and aggravated her as no other had ever done.

And as he filled her, as she cried out in raw ecstasy, a new woman quivered among the ashes of the old.

Six

The slant of the late-afternoon sun found Elizabeth huddled in the room's single armchair, her back to the rays warming the drapes, her bare legs drawn into the circle of her arms. Desperately wishing she smoked—she needed something to calm her chaotic thoughts—she lowered her chin to her knees and watched Dex sleep.

He lay on his side, his tawny hair splayed on the mound of pillows they'd tossed over the mattress in their passion. She'd drawn the sheets to his chin before she'd left the bed, but he'd already disarranged them in his occasional sleepy searches for her beside him. Though he hadn't awakened, his rugged features creased every time his hand met the empty mattress, and she'd held her breath. Awake, Dex was a distraction she hadn't needed or wanted while she'd sorted out the events of the last few hours.

A gentle half-smile pulled at her lips. It was almost worth her affliction to see him so frazzled.

She'd thought him nerveless at one time, invulnerable to the kind of alarm that could turn her own iron-clad mind to oatmeal. But he'd proved otherwise. Because he'd disarmed her, she'd opened herself to the firestorm that had swept over them both. She wanted to hate him for it, to somehow blame him, but she couldn't. He'd held his own with her, giving as well as taking. He wasn't the brute she'd half-convinced herself he was. He was . . . well, he was *Dex*.

Lord, she wished she still disliked him. It would be so much easier.

Impatiently she shoved the regret aside. She'd made her decision; she had to stick to it no matter what the personal cost. The fact that it would be staggering, she blatantly ignored.

The air conditioner whooshed on, stirring the drapes, sending shafts of sunshine frolicking across his eyelids. They fluttered, then flew open, gray eyes focusing on her with disconcerting speed. They warmed with a new light, one that made her feel more naked than she had in the car after the storm. The shattered nerves she'd finally calmed resurfaced with a vengeance.

She tugged the T-shirt over her legs. "Hi."

"Hi, yourself," he murmured. "Are you all right?"

She nodded, her heart catching despite herself. No one's first thought had ever been for her. "Whatever hit me is gone." She shrugged, striving to retain her resolution. "I think it was mostly stress. That's gone too."

He frowned as he rotated his neck. "Why?" He froze in mid-stretch. "The police? Have they—"

She shook her head. "I haven't been cleared. At least, I don't think I have." She lowered her feet to the floor. "For all I know there's a warrant out for my arrest. But as long as I don't know for certain, I'm not doing anything wrong."

He smiled. "Your logic amazes me."

"It's the only way I can handle this whole thing." She stood and moved to the window, her body tense as she peered out at the arrivals in the parking lot. She focused on a balding business-man, standing beside a black Sundance with a ding in the rear bumper. His tie really was dread-ful, and his choice of cars as bland as his face, but he wasn't enough to hold her attention for long, even after he surprisingly moved to the car next to him.

Telling herself to quit stalling, she blurted it out. "I did a lot of thinking, Dex."

She could almost hear the whir of his analytical wheels. "Oh?" he said, the word dripping with suspicion. "About what?"

Her throat convulsed. "The delays. Missing Jane because of them. The real embezzler. The fact that we've reached an impasse." Or turned a corner, she thought. "I don't like being boxed in."

"I know."

"This afternoon I—" She swallowed. "Well, I real-ized tying myself into knots about things I can't change is the surest way to a rubber room, or a hospital. I learned that a long time ago, but I guess I'd forgotten. The only way I can go forward is to stop looking back."

"I know."

Her fingers tightened on the cheap material, wishing he'd stop saying that. "But I don't want a fatality on my conscience."

The silence stretched. "Meaning?"

"Meaning—" She drew a deep breath. "I want you to return to San Francisco."

"I see," he said softly. After an eternal moment, bedclothes rustled. "I think I'd better brush my teeth. That one left a bad taste in my mouth."

She followed, standing outside the doorway as he snatched the needed items from the counter. "You're angry."

"No." The toothpaste squirted to the tile with his force. Ignoring it, he shoved the brush into his mouth. After rinsing, he sighed and leaned against the sink. "No," he repeated, wiping his hands. "I'm not angry. I'm not even surprised, after this afternoon."

A blush crept into her cheeks. "I—wasn't myself."

"That's debatable."

She blinked. "What's that supposed to mean?"

"It's simple." He flung the towel into the tub and crossed his arms over his chest. "This isn't about your conscience. This is all about what happened."

She gaped. "What?"

He nodded. "You're embarrassed!"

"I'm—" She hesitated, his gaze daring her to deny it. "Well, a little, but—"

"You regret that you dropped that corporate armor for a single instant."

"Dex, we acted like a couple of overstimulated teenagers! We didn't even think about the consequences!"

"There hasn't been anyone for a long time," he told her seriously. "I wouldn't take a chance like that with you. I'm healthy as a horse. What about you?"

She hesitated, his confession stirring more than

simple relief. "It's been . . . a long time for me too." She went on quickly. "But that's not the only thing that bothers me."

His voice dropped to a husky murmur. "You hate the fact that you enjoyed every blessed minute of it, don't you?"

She shrugged, tingling all over from the reminder. How did he do that? How could his tone evoke the erotic images of them tangled in the sheets, and on the floor, and . . . "It was a tension release, that's all," she said, attempting to shove the memories far from her consciousness.

He ignored her sulky rationalization, grinning. "It was more than that, and so is your wanting me out of the way. You can't admit that maybe, just maybe, you actually *need* someone's assistance, that this was all a cry for help."

She flinched at the truth. "I didn't *ask* for anything. I *dragged* you into this. I'll never forgive myself for that, Dex. Please don't make it worse than it already is."

"I don't think kidnapping at fingerpoint constitutes coercion. If I remember correctly, I dragged *you* along for the ride."

"It was my idea!"

He shook his head slowly, never breaking eye contact. "It's so like you to take all the credit, isn't it, Hammer? But we don't have time to give out medals now. We have a lot of work to do if we're going to find Jane." He walked past her.

She grabbed his elbow, halting him, glaring at him. For the first time in her life her motives were truly selfless, and he had the gall to doubt her! "This isn't a contest! I don't want you in any more trouble than you already are!"

"Tough."

"Just because we . . . did what we did, it doesn't suddenly make you responsible for me!"

"You can't even say it," he marveled.

She closed her eyes tightly. "We had sex."

"We made love."

Her eyes flew open. "We had sex," she repeated firmly. "Great sex, okay? The ground opened up and swallowed me whole. On a scale of one to ten, it was a fifteen, okay?" She grabbed his arms, longing to wipe the smirk off his face. "But now you're going to get out of the line of fire and go home and work on your little computer!"

His grin widened. "No."

She shook him. "Dammit, be reasonable!"

"No."

A part of her awed mind recognized that she'd finally met the proverbial immovable object. But dammit, she couldn't let him win again! "We're going to settle this."

A long sigh escaped him. Then, quick as thought, he whirled and grabbed her shoulders.

Her head snapped up. Thrown off balance, she steadied herself against his chest. "What are you doing?" she asked, proud of the reasonable tone she could maintain when her toes barely touched the floor. "You realize I could have you singing in the Vienna Boys' Choir in about two seconds."

"Now you listen to me, Beth, and you listen good. It doesn't matter who did what to whom to get us into this, and I don't give a rat's behind for your sudden—and, I might add—your mysterious attack of remorse." He pulled her to within an inch of his face, exasperation clouding his features even as his intense gaze burned into her. "Get this through your thick skull—we're in this together! For better or for worse, in sickness and in health, with or without 'the earth swallowing us whole.' I'm here for the duration. I don't abandon my partner!"

"Partner?" The conviction she read in his eyes disconcerted her, giving her the most ridiculous urge to giggle. "We're not—"

"We're partners," he repeated firmly, his grip easing. "And I hope friends too."

"Friends?" She blinked, feeling something give way inside of her at the hint of uncertainty she heard in his voice. "Are we friends?"

"Of course." He let her slip to the floor but didn't release her. "What else would you call us?"

The question quivered in the air between them. Her gaze traveled over features she knew as well as her own, focused against her will on his mouth, poised millimeters from hers. His thumb began making soothing circles on her skin, which tingled.

"You're so beautiful, Beth," he whispered. "I've never known anyone like you. Don't fight your instincts."

A warm sensation settled in her belly, then exploded and spread to her limbs with astonishing speed. "I don't have instincts," she murmured, her lips caressing his as she spoke, "or friends, either. I work alone."

"So do I. Most of the time."

His breath became hers, his chest skimmed the tips of her breasts. She shivered at the agony of feeling that crashed through her. Against her will, her hand tightened on his sweater and her head drifted back. Weakly, she tried again. "We're complete opposites."

"No." He shifted to her vulnerable throat. "We're too much alike."

"Even worse." His mouth skimmed her neck, then her ear. She was turning that corner again, and panic suddenly flared when she couldn't see around it.

But Lord, he knew exactly what to do to excite her. It was as if he had a magic button that only he could push to make her lose every hard-won ounce of power she had over her universe. And that frightened her more than the police ever had.

"Dex," she said desperately, even as her fingers buried themselves in his hair, "I can't do this."

"Can't?" His teeth grazed her lobe. "Or won't?"

A whimper caught in her throat. "I don't know anymore," she admitted wildly.

He stilled, then drew slowly away, his gaze piercing her soul. She silently implored him to stop, knowing that if he didn't, she wouldn't be able to. And, in typical fashion, Dex saw it.

"Was it that bad?" he murmured.

Unable to draw on any of her old defenses, she could only nod.

He didn't pretend to misinterpret her. She sensed he never had. "We need to change rooms," she whispered.

"For my sake, or for yours?"

She swallowed. "Mine." Tears stung her eyes.

"All right." With a tender smile, he touched one shimmering droplet and brought it to his lips, then to hers. "Now we're blood brothers," he told her solemnly. "Bound to our mutual quest, bed or no bed."

"I thought water wasn't as thick as blood."

He shrugged. "Well, if you have this burning desire to slash your palm open, I think I have a pocketknife somewhere."

His absurdity prompted a chuckle from her. "I'll settle for a tissue and a shower."

Something crossed his face, a ghost of agonized thought. Before she could wonder at it, he ran one finger along her jaw. "You really are beautiful, you know. Your own mother wouldn't recognize you."

"Thanks. I think."

He grinned and flicked a lock of her hair. "I'll see if I can scrounge us up something to eat before I forget my Herculean strength of will and jump you in the tub." He pulled out his wallet and removed several bills, tossing them to the bed. "Go ahead and get us a double, partner." Then he kissed her on the forehead, grabbed the room key from the dresser, and strode from the room, whistling.

Pondering his confusing change of mood, Elizabeth wandered toward the bathroom and flipped on the light beside the sink.

The image in the mirror caught her eye. Vaguely, Elizabeth wondered when a monster had sneaked in. Its dark, graffitied torso perched as if by magic atop stick-figure legs and sled-runner feet. Its mane was a field of blonde bean sprouts, its nose peeled like a birch tree in spring, and someone had flicked Hershey's syrup all over the poor thing's face.

Her mouth curved in a smile. His parting words echoed in her mind. "The man is a master of mood shifts," she told her reflection.

She brushed her wild hair savagely, subduing it by strength of will. She could do nothing about the freckles, but she scrubbed her face until it glowed. She found herself cursing the lack of moisturizer, but her thoughts halted her. She nearly toppled headfirst into the basin when she realized it wasn't finicky pride in her appearance that drove her—it was desire for Dex's approval.

Dismayed, she stared into her own tortured eyes, searching for signs of madness. Is this what two days of stress and a tumble in the sheets did to her? Dex gives her the most exciting time of her life, and suddenly he's Albert Schweitzer, Cary Grant, and St. Jude all rolled into one? What had happened to "arrogant," "overbearing," "infuriating," and "tyrannical"? The man was an intellectual Pershing tank, not a saint!

Where was the woman who'd refused to compromise her goals? she wondered.

She'd lost everything, was the silent reply.

"No," she said aloud. "Not everything." Just her job, her freedom, and possibly her mind, she thought. But she still had her quest.

Her fists clenched. Finding Jane allowed no time to dally with the Spiderman. How could she even *contemplate* repeating their earlier performance? So what if his touch turned her to spaghetti; so what if he had more dimensions than a Heinlein warp—he was a passable companion who occasionally illuminated her investigation, but more often aggravated it. What had happened to her standards? To her authority? What kind of wimp had she become?

The kind he might want? was the silent question.

Elizabeth tossed her head defiantly. She didn't give a hoot in Hanover what Dex thought. He obviously considered her to be some dumb blonde, to be patted on the head and led to bed. Well, she was much, much more than that, and it was time he realized that. She had *no* intention of yielding to those baffling desires. She needed to regain control over her life, and the first step was to take charge of this situation.

A quick glance at her watch told her it was nearly two o'clock, and a Friday. Shaking off the lingering sensation that she had known him forever, she put her mind to work. Of the alternatives they had discussed, only one was viable—even imperative, at this point. Unless she wanted to wait until Monday, she had to get to the school.

But how? The rumpled suit, she determined quickly, would do. She could probably convince the authorities she was a lawyer, or something. But she had no transportation.

Reflected in the mirror, a glint of metal shone beside the dresser. Whirling, she pounced on it, cheering when she realized it was the key ring she'd thrown before they'd—she skittered away from that thought and started her plan in motion.

Fifteen minutes later, Elizabeth the Hammer eased into the driver's seat and switched on the engine. It sputtered, snarled, and then died.

Ice-blue eyes narrowed. "Sheila," she murmured with deadly intent, "you and I are going to have a little talk."

Rejuvenated from his long walk, Dex swung the bag containing their dinner up into his arms as he bounded through the concrete hallway toward their room. She had conceded the awesome poten-

tial of the physical end of their relationship, and
that was more than he'd ever expected. He could
wait for more.

The fact that he wanted more still stunned him,
and he hadn't analyzed his reasons for that desire,
but now he did. He didn't think their lovemaking a
mistake, but he realized it had been a bit prema-
ture. Next time, he wouldn't rush her. If he'd
learned anything about Beth it was that she
couldn't be pushed or bullied even when it was
something she wanted. When forced into a corner,
she simply dug in her heels and resisted.

Rounding the side of the building, he scanned
the parked cars and saw several slots empty. One
in particular niggled at his subconscious, the only
vacant place in the section directly opposite their
room, but before the vague apprehension could
take hold, he noted another, more disturbing
absentee.

Sheila was gone.

His heart launched itself into his throat. Deny-
ing his first thought, telling himself Beth wouldn't
leave voluntarily, he snatched the room key from
his pocket and shoved it into the lock. Visions of
Beth lying unconscious—or worse—in the middle
of the floor invaded his mind. Whispering a silent
prayer, he yanked the door open and cried out her
name, his gaze frantically searching the deserted
room. No body, no sign of struggle. No Beth.

A different kind of fear filled him. Frozen on the
threshold, he swiftly spied the hanger on which
her suit had hung earlier. It was empty. He leaped
toward the dresser, slammed the bag to the surface, and jerked the top drawer out. Her lingerie
had vanished too.

"Damn," he whispered. He'd been wrong, he thought numbly. She'd done it. The minute his back was turned, she'd driven a knife into it. Just the way Amber had.

No, he told himself, surprised that the denial came so quickly, Elizabeth Hamner would never stab anyone in the back. His rational mind added a rueful postscript—of course not; she'd turn the poor sucker around and go for his heart.

Running an agitated hand through his hair, he stormed into the bathroom. There he halted. Her T-shirt and jeans, both damp, decorated the shower rod.

It didn't necessarily mean anything—she hated those clothes—yet the contrary, illogical part of his brain pounced on this evidence. And her toothbrush and pills lying on the countertop reassured him even more. She hadn't deserted him. She'd . . .

She'd what?

Before his inventive imagination could answer the question, he heard a distinctive "roar-putt-putt-cough." He bolted to the door, wrenching it open with such force that the knob punched a hole in the flimsy wall. Uncaring of the damage, he ran to the sidewalk, his gaze on the entrance. The sound grew louder, and within moments, Sheila came huffing and puffing into view.

A bubble of laughter built in his chest as the car halted with a screech of tires, then abruptly surged and overshot her slot. With a snort, she slowly inched backward, hesitating every few inches as Beth positioned her for her own parking place. Dex flinched as Sheila missed a blue Civic by millimeters.

Finally, reluctantly, Sheila crawled into her spot and sputtered to a stop. In the silence that followed, Dex heard Beth's muffled cursing as loudly as a shout. Relief flooded him. She was unharmed.

When the door was flung upward, she exited with all the grace and dignity of a storm trooper. After kicking Sheila's tire, dislodging her chignon in the process, she ripped off her burgundy high-heeled pumps and chucked them inside, then slammed the door shut with the same intensity.

The urge to wrap her in a weeklong bear hug battled an insane need to shake her until her teeth rattled. Defying both, Dex crossed his arms. "Have a nice trip?" he managed calmly.

She whirled around, stomping to him as she flung her arm behind in an accusing point. "I told you she hates me. She did that the whole time!"

No apology, no explanation, not even a touch of remorse. He leaned against the wall. "Maybe she was trying to keep you from doing something stupid. Like leave."

She raised shining eyes to his. "It wasn't stupid, Dex! I think I know where Jane went!"

Dex noticed several guests peering from their windows and doorways, and a dark compact pulling into the lot. He took her arm and dragged her to the room, indicating their audience when she protested.

She quieted immediately, until the door was closed behind them. "Dex, the kids talked about going to visit Daddy, somewhere in Texas, so Jane must have gone—"

"I thought you said she was afraid of her husband."

"She is. But he never hurt her." She blinked,

bewildered. "She told me she was afraid of herself, of loving him so much she'd let him overpower her independence again." She frowned. "It still doesn't make sense."

"And it doesn't prove anything, either," he added. It made perfect sense to him, but he didn't want to give her even more excuses. "She might have told them that to calm their fears."

She shook her head, her zeal back. "That's the last thing she would have told them! Now all we have to do is find some way of confirming it, and I have the perfect plan! When you get into a computer, you can get the bank's phone records too! They keep track of local and long distance, and—"

"So that's where you went? To the school?" His fury rushed to the surface at her blithe assumption that he would share her excitement.

She slumped into the chair by the window. "Of course," she told him, obviously amazed that he hadn't guessed. "I couldn't wait until Monday."

"Could you have waited long enough to leave me a note?" he asked, his voice shaking with suppressed emotion.

She eyed him strangely. "Don't treat me like some erring child, Dexter Wolffe. You waltzed out of here without even considering all the work we have to do."

"And you rushed out without realizing that I might worry about you!"

"Well, I—" She frowned. "I am sorry about that," she murmured. "But Dex, I succeeded! Doesn't that count for something?"

"No," he said, irritated at her. "You dressed up in your business suit, looking exactly like your damned picture! Didn't it occur to you that you might be recognized?" He grabbed her shoulders. "Dammit, didn't you think at all?"

"Obviously not," she said, a dazed grin tugging at her mouth. Elizabeth's mind was a jumble of emotions, but in the forefront was the realization that she'd managed to rattle him again. Had that been a subconscious goal all along? He was still overbearing and arrogant, but he actually cared. "You were worried about me, huh?"

"Of course I was worried!" His voice was as near a shout as she could remember.

"And I've been acting like a spoiled brat." Surprising herself, she admitted that without a qualm.

"Damned straight, you have!"

She pulled the keys from her pocket and held them out. "And you're going to take away my toys and lock me in my room."

Frowning, he released her and took the ring. "Yes," he said, watching her as he would a rabid dog.

Her grin widened. "Anything else, Dad?"

A startled expression flickered across his face, and his mouth pursed as he evaluated her remarks. "I think that about covers it," he said with a nod.

"Good. Do I smell food?" Ravenous now, she followed her nose to the bag on the dresser. "Chinese, my favorite!" Hesitating, she asked him which of the two cartons was his, and he dazedly deferred to her preference.

Still grinning, she handed him a pair of chopsticks, shrugged out of her jacket, and switched on the television, changing the channels until she found an old movie. "*Casablanca!*" she exclaimed, and hurried for a handful of tissues, her eyes narrowing on him as she returned. "If you laugh, just once, you're dead meat." Expertly using her chopsticks, she dug into the spicy Kung Pao shrimp.

He stood staring at her, bemused, for a full minute. Then he shook himself and snatched it from her hands. "Hey!" she cried.

"This," he said, sliding over a second box, "is yours. Nice, bland almond chicken."

She grimaced. "Gee, thanks." When he sat beside her on the bed, he lifted himself, then sat again, a grin spreading over his face. "What?"

"Nothing." He showed her a wad of bills. "I just realized that you didn't get us a double room."

She shivered as that omission took on some major Freudian overtones. Then she shrugged. "I'll sleep in the chair."

"We'll share."

Her hackles went up.

He laughed at her tense posture. "Lord, you have a dirty mind." With the relish she'd begun with, he scooped up his portion of the shrimp. "Personally, I think it's like locking the barn after the horse has escaped, but I have you all figured out, lady."

"Oh?"

"Sure. I watch old movies too. Remember *It Happened One Night*? A wall of Jericho, right down the middle of the bed." He grinned. "It didn't work then, either, but we'll see who breaks first."

Her chin firmed stubbornly. Somehow, again, he'd twisted the conversation to his advantage. She'd resist him easily, she told herself. She'd proven her abilities to her own satisfaction by finding the information at the school all by herself.

If she couldn't do this one little thing, what kind of a commander was she?

Toasting with chopsticks, she accepted his challenge, adding a silent postscript. It was time to give him a taste of his own medicine. And she would hear him admit she was his equal before this trip was over, if it killed her.

The battle began anew.

Seven

Due to their mutual restless night, they both slept late the next morning and barely said a word to each other when they awoke. His walking-on-eggshells attitude solidified her resolution. Dexter Wolffe thought he had her all figured out, did he? The man needed a swift kick in the ego, and she was just the woman to do it.

While Dex went to get breakfast, Elizabeth put the first step of her plan into motion. She showered and scrubbed her skin until it glowed. She could do nothing about her hair's tendency to moppet-curl around her shoulders without the taming of a blow-dryer, but decided it was an asset instead of the liability it had been when she was a child. He had been right about that, though she'd never admit it. Anyone who saw this Shirley Temple version of herself would never believe she was the Hammer. For an instant, panic shivered through her, but she quelled it. It was illusion, after all.

By the time he returned an hour later, carrying a paper bag full of food, she was refreshed and clean and full of a heady, bubbling enthusiasm. She refused to question its source. After days of fear and illness, she'd finally tapped into her natural energy, and that's all that mattered.

As Dex watched, bemused, she bounced onto the newly made bed and dumped her clutch's meager contents to the blanket. "Yes," she hissed, pumping her fist. Elated, she snatched the hairbrush and dragged it through her tangles. When life was stripped to the basics, she decided, one learned to appreciate the *true* luxuries.

She caught him blinking at her, and her enthusiasm subsided. It was time for part two, to stop following and start leading. "We need to take stock," she told him. "How bad is the money situation?"

"Do we have to eat?"

"Figure minimum."

He thought for a moment. "With only gas, motel, and food, we have about four days left."

Unsurprised but disappointed nonetheless, she drew a deep breath and let it out slowly. She hated being dependent on his resources, yet railing against the inevitable only brought pain. There were still options, she decided.

She indicated the bulging sack. "We can't afford any more trips to restaurants, even fast-food places."

"Are you sure?" Dex set two extra-large cups of steaming coffee on the built-in nightstand, then produced three enormous cinnamon rolls, warmed from the coffee's heat, and waved one beneath her nose.

The aroma made her mouth water and her stomach sound like Godzilla's twin brother. Her brush dropped from nerveless fingers. "No doughnut shops either," she said, her words lacking conviction.

"Custard-filled, buttermilk, éclairs, chocolate-glazed . . ." He taunted and hypnotized her with the decadent visions he evoked. "Stick with me, kid, and we could have it all."

His horrible Bogart imitation startled her out of her trance. Shoring up her wavering resolution, she shook her head firmly. "You have no willpower, Spiderman. This is our last indulgence. From now on, it's serviceable calories all the way."

"Spoilsport." Half of his treat disappeared in one bite.

"Philistine," she countered, and cradled her bun in her palms, giving it the respect it deserved. "Alas, poor Yorick, I knew him well." With a sigh of pure ecstasy, she closed her eyes and nibbled at the icing, savoring every blessed molecule.

He sank to the chair, eyeing her with a puzzled smile. "You're in a strange mood."

"I told you, I'm moving forward." She licked a crumb from her fingertip, mentally sticking out her tongue. Take *that*, she thought smugly. "We're going to find Jane, and we're going to clear me of the charges. I feel it in my bones."

He finished his roll and wiped his hands on a napkin. "I thought you had no instincts."

"I don't." She inhaled the scent of her coffee—decaffeinated, no doubt—then sipped. "But the way I see it, we're due for a break." She reached for the second roll. "I hate to admit it, but you were right and I was—I was—"

"Wrong?" he hazarded with raised brows.

Her eyes narrowed. "Yes, I was wr—wr—" She huffed. "I was what you just said."

He snorted, covering it with a long swallow of his coffee. "On which of my many irrefutable points are you willing to make this grand concession?"

She glared at him. "You're going to milk this for all it's worth, aren't you?"

"You bet."

"Fine." Her chin tilted up. "You were right about my anger. It's not worth a stay in the hospital."

He sighed. "I wish I had a tape recorder."

She hid a smile behind the cinnamon roll. She liked this playful side of him, and the one she'd rediscovered in herself. It had been so long since she'd indulged it, she'd nearly forgotten its existence. Besides, he was falling neatly into her trap. "It's silly to rant and rave over things I can't change, so I won't. I'll pretend none of it exists."

He hesitated. "That's not exactly what I meant."

"It's what you do."

"No, I simply don't get angry over every little point."

"You just dissect them."

He sighed. "I'll admit I'm occasionally side-tracked by detail—"

She snorted.

"—but," he went on, "I don't forget the past, I learn from it. I grew up knowing there are certain outside forces I can't control and I go with them, taking them apart to use if necessary. You don't do that. You grind your teeth when you sleep, for Pete's sake. You need to let it go."

"I am. I'm doing something positive instead of dwelling on the negative." Her stomach twinged, as if in denial, and she hauled out the spiral-bound notebook she'd unearthed from the car, determined to advance. She had already proven her point to her satisfaction. She didn't need proof. "We have to plan this carefully."

"No, we don't."

She ignored him and tapped the pencil against her teeth. "You think the key lies in your existing information. I think Jane knows something. If this were a military campaign," she mused, "we would use both our approaches and outflank the enemy. Scissor in from two sides."

He threw up his hands in defeat. "Why do I even bother?"

"I have no idea." She flipped the pages. "Let's get to work and bag us a General."

They spent the rest of the morning and most of the afternoon mapping out their strategy and debating every detail into the ground. Elizabeth suspected Dex did it purposely, but she refused to comment. If he wanted to be a pain in the butt, he was entitled. Lord knew she'd done her share before now. She concentrated on not allowing him to push her into something she might regret, either with their investigation or otherwise.

"In addition to our immediate survival requirements, we need Jane's credit card data, the phone records from the bank, and the list of dummy corporations from your research. One of them will certainly turn up something." She frowned. "It's now Saturday." After jotting down several items, she smiled. "Which means that even in the worst case, I could be cleared by Tuesday! Plenty of time before the money runs out!"

He slapped his head. "I just figured it out!"

"What?"

"You're an optimist!"

"You take that back!"

He laughed.

With a rumble, Elizabeth began her columns of essential needs, possessions, and a wish list, stretching their remaining money to the limit. "Budgeting is my business," she told him. "I might spend it like water sometimes, but I can make the eagle on that last quarter scream for mercy."

He gave her a thoughtful look, but refrained from comment.

This thorough dissection of their finances severely limited their possibilities, but to their mutual surprise, they discovered a wellspring of creativity. "I didn't doubt it for an instant," he told her wryly. "I knew all along you'd make an exceptional crook."

"It's not the inclination, it's the circumstance. If all one has is a shell and a pea," she said philosophically, "one cannot become a plumber."

He winced. "That's ridiculous."

She shrugged. "I'll work on it."

Clothes and food were the easy part. There was a thrift store about a mile from the motel, and it opened at noon on Saturday. Thumbing through the racks of used apparel, she smiled. "There was a time when this was the only place I shopped."

"No money?"

"No taste." Grimacing, she held up an atrocious creation—a skintight dress with a plunging sweetheart neckline, little cap sleeves, and a hem that wouldn't cover a gnat's rear end. "Lime polka dots on white rayon," she said with a sweet smile. "And only one dollar." She looked for a back and couldn't find one. "Gee, it had to cost a whole fifty cents just for all the fabric."

He leered at her. "I like it."

She shot him a dry look and chose a quiet, scoop-necked, pale green T-shirt. When he considered buying a Hawaiian print for himself, she snatched up a red knit shirt and headed for the checkout, leaving him sulking. But not for long.

"What about panties?" he called as he picked up a frothy wisp of black and crimson lace from a table marked "Brand-new." His eyes twinkled. "I like these, honey!"

Every conversation in the place skidded to a halt. Elizabeth's hand froze on her purchases, then she smothered a grin. "They're not your size, *dear*," she cried. A gasp and a snicker filled the ensuing silence. "Besides," she went on innocently as he began to stalk toward her, "you have a closet full of nighties that you *never* wear anymore!"

His gaze narrowed as he obviously fought his laughter. "That's because your leather corsets have crowded them out, tiger lily."

The clerk bagging the shirts gawked.

As Dex neared, Elizabeth noticed that the patrons had inched their way behind him, none actually looking, but all ears aquiver.

Pouting, she ran a finger down his chest and removed all intelligence from her voice. "Oh, stud muffin, you know very well the warrior craze was your idea, not mine." She smugly raised her brows for his benefit, then gave a mournful sigh for the clerk's. "But if you have your heart set on the panties, I guess they could be a late Christmas present. They are your color, after all."

His wicked glint was a warning, but she had no time to react. One moment she was standing beside him, congratulating herself for getting the last word, the next she was arched backward over the counter, pretzeled in Dex's arms, his face a whisper from hers. Pinned to the Formica, she could only swallow hard.

"Your real Christmas present was enough, my little fire-eater," he murmured hoarsely. "Your incredible body, wrapped in nothing but that big, golden ribbon." He groaned. "You certainly lifted my holiday spirits."

He kissed her, hard and fast, igniting every atom in her body. Then he straightened them both and calmly asked the sputtering clerk the cost of the clothes. Dex tossed down the amount, picked up the bag, and held open the door for her.

Elizabeth staggered, met the gaze of a patron fanning himself with his wife's purse, and felt the heat flare in her cheeks. "Cute," she muttered as she bolted past Dex. "Very cute."

He grinned. "I thought so."

On the walk back to the car, she realized she couldn't let him retain the upper hand. Ruthlessly, she ignored her reaction to his performance and directed him to the local supermarket; once there, she turned the conversation to their plans. "We could go back to Jane's house," she suggested. "Talk to the neighbors."

"What makes you think they know anything when the people at the school didn't? And supposing they know something, why would they tell you?"

"I could pretend to be Jane's sister."

"What does she look like?"

She sighed, feeling her scheme crumble. "Jane's five-foot-zip, brown hair, brown eyes, and she has a distinct mustache."

Dex eyed her Nordic fairness and his mouth twitched. "Your logic impresses me more each time."

She huffed. She couldn't give up now! "A late census-taker then. Anything." She carried the grocery bag to the car, set it on the floor, then rummaged around the clutter. "All I need is a clipboard and my suit, and they'll be putty in my hands."

"No clipboard, Beth."

"I'll think of something." Her burgundy shoes were where she'd left them the day before, in no need of cleaning, so she dropped them back among the wrappers, felt-tip markers, and soda cans. She studied the collection with a sigh as Dex pulled into the motel lot and switched off the engine. "Why don't we clean out this mess?"

"What mess?" he asked artlessly.

A glare of green and white, hidden beside the driver's seat, caught her eye. She gasped. Picking up the dress with two fingers, she flagged him. "How the hell did you manage to sneak this past me?"

"You were easy to distract."

She opened her mouth, then decided it wasn't worth the energy; she'd let him think he won this little battle while she focused on her subversive war. Picking up their purchases, she strode to their room, scanning its neatness. "Too bad the maid doesn't do cars," she muttered, her eagle gaze spying the one piece of clutter. She pounced on the tiny gum wrapper.

"What's that?" he asked, amused by her attention to detail.

She sniffed it. "Peppermint." She balled it up and hurled it at the trash can. "Cheap motel, shoddy service." Then she set the bags on the dresser and handed him his shirt, determined to complete the strategy for locating Jane before they made a single move.

After changing into their "new" clothes, she fixed bologna sandwiches and apples, her brain whirling with possibilities for their next step, acquiring a computer. But at every point, she found herself stonewalled. In addition to the exorbitant rates the local companies wanted for renting one, Dex was concerned about bypassing their security systems.

"But you wrote the program!" she exclaimed, confused.

He nodded and sat on the edge of the bed. "Yes, I did."

"You're that good, huh?"

He shrugged. "The government's been after me for years to head up a security task force. They seemed to think I could have stopped that multimillion-dollar theft a couple of years ago."

"Could you?"

He pondered the question. "Stop it, maybe. Prevent it, definitely. But I wasn't too tactful with my refusal, which is why they took me off your case. I, uh, don't like suits."

"I noticed. Why?"

He glanced away. "I got into a tangle with my bosses over a program someone stole from me and labeled her own. They believed her until I proved them wrong. That's why I left the corporate world, really."

"Her?" Suddenly his antagonism made sense, she thought. This "her" had hurt him badly. But before she could pursue that elusive line of thought, his gray eyes glittered with predatory intent. She tensed.

"None of that's important now," he told her, stretching out beside her. "Even if we could afford a portable computer, I would need extra equipment to defeat the motel's phones. As it is now, I think I can bypass the callback line of defense in my system, but it could take hours. These phones are run by computer, too, to switch from the desk to the room. There's always a chance of glitching the information. That's assuming they're even compatible in the first place."

"We don't have much choice." She jumped as his arm brushed hers. Briefly she wished she'd chosen the Hawaiian print. The red polo shirt stuck to his broad shoulders like hot glue and brought out the deeper highlights in his tawny hair. Averting her eyes, she inched away and tapped her pencil against her teeth. "What's a 'callback?'"

He reached up to halt her nervous movement. "You're tangling yourself up again. It doesn't have to be this complicated."

"I'm not, and it's not." She irritably flipped the pencil. It arrowed across the room and left a tiny graphite mark on the wall. "What's a 'callback?'" she repeated.

He chuckled and gave up the argument. "Initial block to any would-be thief, after passwords." He shifted to his side. "My computer calls the bank's computer. The bank asks who it is, checks its memory for the name, then hangs up and calls back." His elbow grazed her breast. "If that person isn't at the correct phone number, they can't get in."

"That's"—her breath caught—"ingenious," she finished weakly.

He waved off her praise. His hand landed on her thigh. "It's standard. But it's one way I suspected this embezzlement was an inside job. As I said, though, it's minor." He leaned over to read her list, and his fingers slipped along the inseam of her jeans. "And unless you have another notebook—a big one—we'll need a printer."

Swallowing hard, she bit back a moan and searched his face for any sign that his erotic fondling was intentional.

"Is anything wrong?" he asked.

"No." She slid to the floor and crossed to the dresser, folding her old T-shirt with meticulous precision. "Any old friends in Phoenix? One that owes you a *biiig* favor?"

He joined her, leaning to drape his sweater over the mirror and hand her the projectile pencil. "I'd have hit him up for money long before now if I did." He pressed the length of his body against her spine.

She skittered under his arm. "Dex?" Her voice squeaked. She cleared her throat and sidled into the chair. Dammit, even now that she knew the chase was deliberate, she couldn't find it in herself to tell him to end it. Her only chance was to divert him as he was trying to divert her. "Is there any possibility that you'll trip one of the other alarms?" she asked desperately. "I mean, you said my signature was all over the transactions and the FBI will be monitoring the bank's computers. Won't everybody and his brother be alerted not only to your intrusion, but to you?"

"That's a chance we have to take," he explained with a distracted smile. "Sometimes you have to trust your instincts, Beth."

The problem was, the things her "instincts" told her were irrational and impossible under the circumstances. It didn't matter that Dex was the sexiest man she'd ever met. His amorous bent was obviously his reaction to the challenge of the chase. And her response wasn't unusual at all—she'd simply transferred her monetary dependence to her emotions, where she could control them. Unfortunately, she was finding it more and more difficult to keep her libido in check, and was fast becoming hooked.

But she couldn't let him win. Thinking quickly, she asked, "Okay, if we can't access anything from here, then where? A computer store won't let you walk in and use their phone, not if you're not buying." She rubbed her face, keeping a wary eye on Dex. "The bank?"

"Too risky." He edged toward her.

She gulped. "Any business has its own computer these days. Dress up like—" Too complicated, she thought. Keep it simple, find the obvious. "The school had one, maybe—"

She cut herself off as it struck her like a bucket of cold water. "Not one computer, Dex. A place with dozens!" She'd effectively halted his pursuit. "Printers, modems, everything your little heart desires, and access to a nationwide mainframe." She leaned forward. "The university!"

"That's like using an elephant gun to kill a butterfly, but we have no choice, do we?" Wry amusement flashed in his eyes. "Couldn't you have figured this out five minutes later?"

"I'd say my timing was impeccable."

Reluctantly, he reached out to help her from her chair, shaking his head. "Why didn't I think of it before?"

"Because your brains are in your jeans," she muttered, and grabbed her purse.

"Actually," he said as he held the door open, "they've been in yours."

She refused to dignify that with a comment.

Screened by a scrawny bush in a built-up planter in the middle of the quad, Elizabeth and Dex studied the area before them, devising their plan of attack. They couldn't waltz in, as she'd hoped. The place was a fortress, with its own resident dragon.

The sign on the double glass doors read "Computer Lab, Students and Faculty Only." Inside, on the white corridor wall, a placard indicated the advanced-systems area and the general lab, with arrows in opposite directions. Beneath this stood a desk, with warnings posted in red, "ID and/or class slip required for admission."

Their dragon sat behind the desk, guarding the entrance.

He was a pimple-faced male dressed in baggy jeans, horn-rimmed glasses, and a T-shirt that proclaimed "Violators Will Be Shot."

Elizabeth glanced at Dex with a dry smile. "Add

a pocket protector, and that's how I'd imagined you would look."

"That *is* how I used to look," he countered.

She blinked. "You're kidding."

"Nope. I couldn't buy a date until I got on the football team, and even then I was too short, too skinny, and too involved in my studies."

"The girls in your school were idiots," she said firmly.

He glanced at her in surprise. "Yeah?"

"Sure," she told him. "Anyone with half a brain knew to date the eggheads." Her eyes twinkled. "With a few notable exceptions, they're all loaded now." Before he could comment, she hushed him and pointed.

A lanky teenager in a letter jacket strode through the doors and handed their adversary a card. The dragon examined it with an intensity that should have bored a hole right through the plastic. After a moment, he shook his head and pointed toward the general lab. A small argument ensued, ending when he picked up the phone and waved it in a threatening manner. His lips formed the dreaded word, "Security." The jock stomped out, and the kid smiled smugly.

Dex viewed this performance with a jaundiced eye, then sank to the retaining wall. "Eddie McDermott," he said with a groan.

"Who?" Elizabeth sat beside him, shoving her increasingly wayward hair from her brow. "Dex, do you know him?"

"Not exactly." He sighed. "But every school has an Eddie McDermott. You know the type—the hall monitor that made a rottweiler look like a Yorkshire terrier? President of every club that no one wanted to join in the first place? Kissed the principal's—"

"I get the picture."

He nodded, grinning reminiscently. "He's probably still managing that fast-food restaurant."

"Or is vice president of a bank," she murmured. She saw Dex's startled glance and felt heat creep into her cheeks, then moved along before he could comment. "There's no cover to sneak past him, and even if you did, it's not so busy that he couldn't catch you at a terminal." She chewed her lip. "We have to create a diversion."

"And you do that so well."

Ignoring him, she narrowed her eyes on the knots of students who had drifted into the quad. The boys, with their overactive glands, hooted at every woman they saw. The girls stood in bunches, giggling and whispering secrets, or disdainfully ignored the juvenile males and went on with their business.

Freshmen, she thought wryly. Typical Saturday evening on campus.

Dex rose. "While you're working on your strategy, I'm going to talk my way inside."

She stood. He pushed her back. Her chin tilted upward. "I'm going with you."

He shook his head. "Beth, what you know about computers wouldn't fill your notepad. I'm the logical choice to handle this one. Here." He handed her his keys. "You go back to the car and wait for me. And keep your eye out for uniforms!" He kissed her cheek and strode away.

"Hey!" She sprang to her feet, but he'd already pushed through the doors and breezed by "Eddie." Furious that he'd twisted their partnership once again, determined not to let him rule, she began to follow.

She halted abruptly as the kid reached for the phone almost before Dex had spoken a word. Dex stopped and spread his hands wide, his best innocent expression firmly in place as he edged back to the desk.

A smirk spread across her face and she crossed her arms over her chest. Dexter Wolffe, the master of conceit, was striking out. "Serves you right," she muttered, relishing every instant.

Dex patted his pockets and shrugged. The kid shook his head and pointed to his watch. Elizabeth briefly checked the lab's hours, which were far from over, then decided she didn't care what he was saying. She wanted to kiss him for popping Dex's self-righteous bubble.

Then she frowned. As much as she was enjoying the situation, it wasn't helping them find Jane. The only way to do that, of course, was to go back to *her* original idea. She needed a diversion. And Dex might just have given her the means to create it.

A devilish smile replaced the smirk. With a last, wickedly appreciative glance at Dex, who now stood stiffly in a battlelike posture, she tossed the keys in the air, caught them, and hurried back to Sheila.

Once inside, she considered the Peterbilt hat, his glasses, the blanket, the felt-tip markers; then she leaned to the driver's side and found the dress she'd once thought too flashy to ever consider wearing. Now, she decided happily, it was perfect. As she straightened, her gaze swept the litter on the floor and in the narrow space behind the seats, searching for any other useful item.

She found more than she'd bargained for. Wedged between the passenger seat and the discarded bumper, she saw a lump of pale leather, a very distinct shade of tan that she remembered well. She breathlessly pulled at it, jerking it free of its tight prison.

It was her wallet.

Hand trembling, she opened it and counted the bills, which had hardly seemed adequate three days ago. Now the money felt like a fortune! A glorious smile lit her face as she realized they wouldn't have to pinch pennies. No more bologna, she thought happily. No more thrift-shop discards. No more cheap motels with hard mattresses—heck, no more single rooms!

Her smile faded at this reminder. No more Dex a breath away, to irritate and frustrate her, to tantalize and seduce her. No more challenge of making something out of nothing. And no more reason to continue her plan for Dex's downfall.

The money represented the easy way, and that was a road she'd never taken in her life. Dexter Wolffe needed to realize that she was not a woman to be coddled, protected, and underestimated, and he wouldn't learn his lesson if she gave him the means to start all over again.

Without examining any hidden motivation, she shoved the wallet back into its hiding place. This time, she decided, the situation would be on her terms.

Besides, she thought, she owed him a rescue.

Eight

After a quick scan of the parking lot to make sure no people were in view, Elizabeth remembered that Sheila's windows were tinted anyway, so she shimmied out of her shirt, then her bra, and slipped the dress over her head. To her surprise, it was snug in places nothing had ever been tight before. She skinned off her jeans and picked up her burgundy heels. They weren't bright enough, but in the absence of anything gaudier, they would have to do.

Tilting down the passenger visor, she found the mirror, then scrounged through her purse. In addition to her lip balm, the only things she carried were dark mascara, lipstick in a muted shade of wine, and a tube of coverup. Though it was sufficient for an executive, it wouldn't do at all for the "distraction" she envisioned. But she would think of something.

After rubbing a thin layer of the light makeup over her freckles, she rummaged on the floor and rose with a rubber band and two markers, one a fine-tipped watercolor black, the other a red. "Perfect," she muttered.

Expert hands applied the liner to her lids, smudged it into the crease with a wet finger, and brushed color on her lashes. She then drew in a cherry-red mouth and pouted her lips, gratified with the result. The face in the mirror was startling, to say the least, but if she got the job done, who cared if she looked like a streetwalker?

A tiny frown marred her brow as she studied the image. Wavy, pale blonde hair, even lighter from exposure to the desert sun, tumbled over her cheeks. Too-large features stood out boldly, seeming erotic rather than unfashionable. For the second time in as many days, Elizabeth stared at herself and marveled at the unfamiliar woman who stared back. She was going to knock his analytical mind into the ozone, she thought, and a rush of warmth pooled in her stomach as she realized the unidentified "him" didn't wear horn-rimmed glasses.

Before she caught herself, she wet her lips with her tongue, the movement startling her out of the thought. Remembering the ease with which the liner had smeared, she inspected her tongue, expecting to see it coated with the crimson dye. It was its normal color. Dismayed, she checked the label and realized she'd coated her lips with permanent marker.

This was not a good omen.

Shaking herself, she decided it didn't matter, and pulled half her hair into the rubber band on top of her head. With a last, assessing look at the bimbo in the mirror, she centered the cascade of curls, shoved her bare feet into her shoes, tweaked the cap sleeves over her shoulders, and, less than five minutes after she'd entered, exited Sheila.

When she stood she found yet another problem. The dress that she'd laughingly stated wouldn't cover a gnat's rear end barely covered hers. At her first long pace, it slid up past her panties. She tugged it down, and her neckline dove to her navel. She hauled it back up and exposed an inch of pink. "This is ridiculous," she murmured.

Drawing a deep breath, which several pairs of hidden eyes thoroughly enjoyed, she arranged the garment to accommodate her modesty and reined in her tendency to stride. She'd always wondered why the women who dressed this way didn't walk like normal human beings; now she knew. If they didn't mince their steps, they'd be arrested for indecent exposure!

She practiced wriggling her backside as she stepped through the lot, and had to twitch her hem down again. Engrossed in maintaining her disguise, she didn't hear the trio of soulful sighs.

Step, wiggle, tug; lick lips, ruffle hair, cover breasts, pull hem down . . . By the time she reached the quad, she had it down to a rhythm that she chanted like a mantra, with an occasional reminder to smile thrown in for good measure. Soon she would prance into that lab and distract that idiot at the desk, leaving the field wide open for her computer expert to do all the accessing his devious little heart desired.

A wolf whistle pierced the air. Smiling at the unfamiliar tribute, she paused and glanced over her shoulder.

Half the football team stood twenty feet behind her, applauding.

Her amusement faded, but it was too late. At her apparent encouragement, they sauntered toward her. She drew herself up and gave them her best glacial glare. Labeling her a "wildcat," they kept their distance, but their vocal appreciation escalated. Suddenly, the chase was on.

Swearing, Elizabeth headed toward the lab triple-time. Unlike a certain drunken Marine, they had nothing more dangerous than harassment in mind, she realized, but their timing stunk. She cursed herself for not taking the juvenile crowd into account. She could hear the thud of their steps trailing, and her pace increased.

The double glass doors stood before her. Dex sat on the edge of the desk, speaking to someone out of view, and if she hadn't been preoccupied she might have noticed that his posture was no longer hostile and ready for battle. But she chose that moment to peek behind her, and found that the slavering pack's numbers had doubled—a fraternity had joined the hunt.

When she turned back to the lab, she saw that Dex had noticed the activity outside. He looked as if he'd swallowed his teeth, and this filled her with perverse satisfaction. Wide-eyed, he glanced at the unseen aide, then back at her. He gave a shake of his head and unobtrusively waved her away.

Her fists clenched and she glared, challenging his so-called authority. Damning his hotdogging instincts, she wet her lips, shook her hair back, plastered an empty-headed smile on her face, and swept inside, searching for her target.

He was gone. In his place stood a rigid, businesslike brunette. And she wasn't amused.

Her thick brows lifted. Elizabeth's jaw dropped. Dex's gray eyes howled with unholy delight. Elizabeth groped for something—anything—to say to get her out of this mess.

Then all hell broke loose as the pack found its quarry.

In the ensuing chaos, she met Dex's gaze for a single, eternal moment, stunned by the unexpected admiration and the unguarded desire that fired his eyes beneath the laughter. Suddenly, she didn't feel the jostling of too many people in too small a space, nor even the pinch from an over-eager student. She didn't hear the aide's shrieks for order. Elizabeth was alone with Dex. His laughter became hers, transformed with wonder and warmth into something magical, something miles above this farce.

Something *shared.*

And Beth knew without a doubt that the research would confirm her suspicions as to Jane's whereabouts, and that it was more than having no one else to run to. She hadn't understood until now that Jane had finally quit fighting this overwhelming emotion. She'd gone *home.*

As she swayed against the desk, dazed by the revelation, Dex blew her a kiss and slipped away in the confusion.

Nearly two hours later, Dex emerged into the hallway with a stack of printouts, whistling, feeling as if he had received the Nobel Prize yet not understanding why. The file-accessing process had been remarkably easy, true, but the information he'd found was nebulous at best—it wouldn't account for his buoyant, victorious mood. He decided that not only would he not question it, but he would walk straight past the guardian of the gate.

As he neared, he saw that the crowd had dispersed, leaving an odd, echoing silence. Only the female at the desk remained, her head pillowed on her arms. When she heard his footsteps, she glanced up, startled, looking like Atlanta after Sherman had marched through. Her eyes were smudged and rather haunted, her hair had exploded from its tight bun, her neat blouse and skirt were distinctly diagonal.

He grinned at her. "Rough night?"

Automatically she opened her mouth to tell him off, saw the printouts, hesitated, and reached for the security phone instead. She paused again, regarding his unrepentant expression.

Then she threw up her hands. "Hell with it. Take the blasted things." She shoved more papers his way. "Take the whole lab, for all I care!"

"Thanks," he told her. "This is all I want." He turned toward the double doors. "By the way," he called over his shoulder, "you should always wear your hair down like that." He spun and lowered his voice. "It makes you look mysterious."

"Really?" she asked, touching the straggling strands wistfully. "Me?"

"Really. You." At her tenuous smile, he pushed through the doors into the dusky evening, feeling even more pleased with himself.

His zest stumbled a bit when he slid into the car. Beth sat in the passenger seat, staring through the windshield at the Technicolor sunset that only desert air could produce. It glowed through the glass, firing her unbound ashen hair with orange, warming the color of her dress to emerald. His gaze wandered over her costume, lingering on her breasts, on the incredible length of smooth leg she had neatly folded at the ankles; then he touched the full, scarlet lips. Heat suffused his limbs at the erotic picture she presented.

He quelled it. Lust was a part of his feelings for her, but he needed more from her than the animal passion they'd shared once already. He didn't know what had passed between them at the lab, but he knew in a blinding flash that whatever it was, it had caused his jaunty mood, and that it was something he couldn't rush. Resisting the urge to snatch her into his arms and kiss her senseless, he tossed the printouts into her lap.

She jumped and glanced at him, quickly lowering her gaze to the papers. "Anything?" she asked in a distracted tone.

"Maybe." He switched on the engine and pulled out of the lot. "The credit cards were a bust; the dummy corporations add only a few to the ones I already gave you."

Her blue eyes sharpened. "And the phone list?"

"Ah, that was interesting. Lots of local calls, but," he added, "there *were* a few long-distance ones."

She continued to gaze at the sunset, swiveling her head around to follow it when he turned onto the street. "Unfortunately, that's not unusual. Most would go to their 800 line, but a few the office would handle personally."

"Oh." When she made no move to study the lists, he frowned. "Don't you want to look through the printouts?"

"Later." She folded her hands over the papers, watching as he deftly maneuvered through the slow-moving traffic. "Did you know the Phoenix natives call these people 'snowbirds'? They come during the winter; tourists and seasonal inhabitants. The town nearly doubles this time of year."

He shot a quick, puzzled glance her way. "No, I'd never heard that."

"The desk clerk told me." She indicated the sky with a nod of her head. "Some clouds moving in over there. Think we might have rain?"

"I don't know." Dex's skin tingled from the undercurrents he suddenly felt in her conversation. Her voice, lowered to a husky purr, and her body, prudishly stiff yet clothed like a wanton, gave him the disturbing sensation that he'd walked into an electrical storm or a David Lynch film. He tried to find a common thread of logic in her words, but found none; yet he couldn't shake the feeling that this wasn't filed under the same heading as peacock sneezes and budgeting. As straightforward as Beth was about almost anything under the sun, she shied away from emotional issues, choosing the roundabout instead of the direct. But she wasn't trying to distract him this time, she was leading. To what?

"Are you worried about a delay?" he asked, voicing what he considered her paramount concern.

"No," she said, surprising him. "Wherever Jane is, she'll be there tomorrow, or the next day. She feels . . . safe, I think." She pushed her hair back but didn't fuss with it when it cascaded forward again. "She has reason. No one but me is really after her."

"*We* are."

A tiny smile touched her ruby lips. "*We* are after her." She lowered her gaze to her hands. "I'm not used to that. Having a 'we' instead of a 'me,' I mean."

"I know," Dex caught his breath at her confession. It was only another step, but it was a big one. He waited for her to say more, but she sat in silence for the remainder of the drive, staring at the pattern her tightly interlaced fingers made against her dress.

As he drove into the motel parking lot, she spoke again, startling him with her statement. "I'm selfish, Dex." Her words seemed to tumble out. "And I'm moody. And stubborn, don't forget that. And . . ." She groped for another adjective.

"Pushy?" he supplied with a twinkle, attempting to lighten her self-defamation.

Her eyes narrowed. "Determined," she said firmly. Then a ghost of a frown flickered over her brow. "No, I am pushy, aren't I?"

His heart melting into a puddle, he switched the engine off and turned to face her. When she refused to meet his gaze, he pulled her hands into his, gently unraveling the knot of fingers. Pretty speeches weren't his style, but neither were they hers. "Beth, I won't lie to you. You're all those things. So am I, for that matter. But you're also sensitive when you allow it, intelligent when you have to be, generous when you forget your corporate responsibilities, and you can laugh at yourself when you let your guard down."

One corner of her mouth lifted. "Talk about honesty," she muttered.

"Are you fishing for compliments?"

Her grip tightened and she lifted her blue eyes to his. "No, Dex. I don't fish."

His throat tightened as he saw the glisten of tears. "I know, honey." Tenderly, he brushed the corner of her eye with his thumb. "But you haven't figured out that you don't have to. Not with me, and not with anyone else who knows you."

She leaned into his caress for a moment, her eyes squeezed shut. "That's the problem, isn't it?" she murmured, then pulled herself away. Without further explanation, she slipped out of the car and stood waiting by the motel room door.

Baffled and more than a little frustrated by her abrupt shift, Dex gathered the printouts and left Sheila. After he'd let them into the room, he set them carefully on the dresser, watching Beth as she strode toward the bathroom, walking out of her shoes as she went. The dress crawled up her hips, but she seemed not to notice. Unfortunately for his resolution, every male hormone in his body did.

He tried to reason with them. He sensed that she was wavering on some precipice and he didn't want to push her off prematurely, but he couldn't concentrate on the reasons he *shouldn't*. His rationality wasn't exactly at an all-time high. When she exited and leaned over the sink, splashing and soaping her face, he swallowed back a moan at the sight of her perfect, rounded buttocks, outlined in pink lace.

It was too late for logic. Instincts older than time and stronger than his own took control.

As she toweled off her face, he stood behind her, millimeters from touching her. Her startled gaze met his in the mirror, and she froze. "Dex?" she whispered.

He opened his mouth to speak but couldn't. Now that he'd made the decision, paradoxically, he wanted to prolong it. No hot rush to the pinnacle, as it had been before. He didn't want to give her an excuse to pull away again. His fingers itched to stroke the length of skin exposed by the backless scrap of cloth, his tongue ached to touch the spot at the base of her neck that he had learned drove her into a frenzy. But for now it was enough to caress her with his gaze, and his eyes zeroed in on her lush, ruby lips.

She followed his direction. "The color won't come off," she said. "I—I used permanent marker."

He wanted to offer to chew it off, but instead leaned over to the first aid kit, never breaking the reflected eye contact. His fingers closed on the small bottle of rubbing alcohol. He eased a tissue from the dispenser beside her and poured the liquid into the thirsty paper.

When she began to turn, he shook his head. Reaching around her, avoiding any other contact, he gently wiped her mouth, which parted automatically for his ministrations. Red stained the tissue, but he barely noticed. His entire being focused on the throbbing pulse at her temple, the sharp movement of her breasts as her breathing quickened, the telltale pucker of skin beneath her bodice. Exquisite agony ripped through him when she didn't resist him. This time, he vowed, it would be perfect.

Beth felt her nipples harden against the silky fabric, felt the caress of the tissue over lips that pulsed in rhythm with the blood that pounded in her ears. She felt herself lured by sleepy eyes that somehow saw into her soul, intense gray eyes that promised pleasures beyond those she'd already found with him, and she was captured in the emotion he poured through that fragile, ephemeral contact.

No matter how many times she'd told herself this mystic bond would disappear once they returned to reality, she hadn't convinced her heart—or her body. Her need for him went beyond all reason. No matter how she'd tried to fight it, the wistful, lonely part of her whispered that this man's perception went beyond mundane facts to the woman she might have been, seducing her with possibilities.

Would it be so wrong to be that woman for one more night?

She felt him replace the tissue with a warm washcloth, cleansing the bitterness, somehow washing away a lifetime of suspicion.

When he drew it off, she reached up and caught his fingers in hers. Swallowing hard, she blinked her misty vision clear and met his gaze firmly in the mirror. He stilled, his eyes darkening as she replaced the cloth on her lips, then drew it over her chin, down the length of her throat, and lower. She felt the trickle of water between her swollen breasts, the rough graze of terry along her sensitized skin, the brush of him, hard and ready, against her buttocks. A long, trembling shudder ripped through him, telling her more than mere words ever could.

This heady evidence of her power over him made her reel. It didn't matter that he had given her that authority. She realized she was giving him the same power over her, and for the first time in her life it didn't frighten her. Against her better judgment, defying all the facts that told her it could never work, the Hammer had fallen in love with the Spiderman. Tomorrow she would analyze it, but tonight she needed to experience it.

With only a slight hesitation, she tossed the

cloth aside and guided his fingers to her shoulder, hooking them under her dress and abandoning him to his own initiative.

He slid the sleeve to her elbow, exposing one coral-tipped breast. With a sharp, indrawn breath, he cupped it, his large, sun-darkened hand an erotic contrast on her pale skin. His thumb teased the hardened nipple to full erection, the visual movement exciting her as much as the physical clutch she felt deep within her. She eased her hands behind her, digging her nails into his buttocks, pulling the hard length of him to her even as she arched into his touch.

Partners share, she reflected fleetingly, and it was her last thought before she surrendered to sensation, and to this new, overwhelming emotion.

Dex watched, mesmerized, as her eyelids drifted half-closed and her head fell back to his chest. In a rush of desire, he realized with amazement that she'd not only relinquished her command, but had placed her trust in his abilities.

For an instant, that realization made him clench; then she writhed along his engorged manhood, making him dizzy with need, chasing his own ghosts into purgatory. They were perfect together, and he knew it. He burned to bury himself in her, to quench the firestorm that raged inside of him. But he couldn't, not yet. He wanted her to know exactly what she'd invited, to finish the seductive torture she'd started.

With the weight of her breast in one hand, he used his other to tug at her panties until they slipped beyond the view of the mirror. Quickly, before he lost his resolve, he pushed the opposite sleeve over her arm, then shoved the gaudy fabric to her waist, and farther, until it disappeared. The mirror showed only a peek of pale curls at the bottom, and he stepped back to exhibit the full effect to her.

Her blue eyes fluttered but stayed open, unable to deny the sight of her body, naked in the harsh overhead light, pressed into his. Her chest heaved with the tiny sighs that crept from her throat.

He dared not watch any longer, knowing if he did, he would spin out of control. With a groan, he buried his face in her subtly scented hair, finding the base of her neck by feel more than by actual direction. He nipped at the tender skin, reveling in the shiver that rippled over her. Then his free hand crept over her belly, sliding over silky curls into the moist heat between her thighs, gently rubbing his palm over the sensitive, hardened flesh as his fingers continued to circle her nipple.

Intent on her pleasure, he lost himself in her. They were no longer man and woman; he could not perceive where she began and he ended. Her body was molded to his, and he felt every shiver of her building ecstasy as sharply as he felt his own.

Suddenly her body went rigid, her grip on him becoming almost painful. Her breast surged into his hand. Then she called out, a triumphant, ringing shout of elation, a cry that he echoed, muffled by her wild mane, though his release was emotional, not physical.

That release was yet to come. Driven half-mad by her uninhibited delight, he swept her around and crushed his hungry mouth to hers, the contact gentling almost immediately as hunger became tenderness. Her tongue intertwined with his, tasting, imprinting senses in a quest for more than this shadow play of intimacy. Their breath became one, their hearts beat in a single cadence, their figures danced to the precise, loving rhythms ordained only by instinct.

Neither knew whose fingers unfastened, whose hands brushed clothing aside as obstacles, and neither cared. Together, they lowered themselves to the bed. Together, they cried out as their bodies thrust to join in the most intimate display of all, their gazes locked, exhibited to none but their hearts and souls.

And finally, when the duel pleasure built to the breaking point, a single voice caroled their rapture.

Much later, after the ebb and flow of passion had manifested itself in another prolonged tide of loving, when their internal time clocks struck the dead of night, he held her close. Longing to let loose the words he'd held in for what seemed an eternity, he opened his mouth to tell her of his love.

Before he could speak, she chuckled. "I wish you could have seen your face when I walked into that lab," she told him.

Her uncanny ability to sense the emotional issues unnerved him at times, and her abrupt mood changes disconcerted him. But he'd learned not to try and analyze her. He trusted his instincts, and right now they demanded patience. There was more than one way to express his feelings, and until they found their way out of this labyrinth, he would have to be content with following her lead.

He smiled at her in the darkness. "I wish you could have seen *your* face when you saw that poor girl. Those guys were a stroke of genius, though."

"They were an accident. I was trying my best Marilyn Monroe imitation, and I ended up as the Pied Piper."

He caressed her hip possessively. "I think we should burn that dress."

"I like it," she said, pouting, then ran her tongue over his ear, the small gesture firing his passion yet a third time, chasing all thoughts from his mind but one. "Naughty," she whispered, giggling as his reaction became evident. "We should stop now and get some sleep. We have a lot to do tomorrow."

"Why?" He forced himself to concentrate on her statement, but her touch did the most bizarre things to his thought processes.

She stroked the inside of his high. "Because I know where Jane is."

"You do?" Somehow that revelation didn't excite him at all. Then again, he didn't think a nuclear explosion would have diverted him at this point. "You didn't look at the printouts."

"I don't have to. She's in Galveston, with her ex-husband. I have a hunch one of those long-distance phone numbers begins with four-oh-nine."

"Hunch? You?" He closed his eyes tightly as her nimble fingers teased his most sensitive flesh. "I admire that in a woman," he murmured, his voice cracking.

Her lips closed over his nipple, and she sucked. "Do you know what I admire about you?"

"What?" he said with a gasp, rolling her beneath him.

"Your stamina," she whispered.

Nine

Despite their best intentions, by midmorning they were only halfway between Phoenix and Tucson. It was Beth's fault, and she knew it, but she couldn't seem to help herself. She should be happy that the phone records had confirmed her suspicions, that one of the long-distance numbers turned out to be the ex-husband's bait shop in Galveston. She should be cavorting like an idiot, celebrating their first real lead.

"By tomorrow morning," Dex told her cheerfully, "we should be shaking hands with your witness."

Beth's stomach knotted. "We'll see," she said, pretending it was caution that tempered her excitement.

She turned away, avoiding the intense gray eyes that always seemed to perceive her thoughts. It made no sense, but no matter how she tried to deny it, she hadn't wanted to leave Phoenix.

When Dex had hurriedly checked them out of their room, she'd found herself lingering in the shower, dithering over their meager belongings, and debating her preference between the pale green T-shirt or the dark one he'd bought on the road. With his usual élan, he'd simply stuffed his sweater, her suit, and his erstwhile joke into a paper bag, then slipped his red polo shirt over his head and walked out the door.

After she'd convinced him to stock up on food for the drive, she wandered the supermarket like a professional bargain-hunter, comparing everything from price to weight. She'd even attempted to convince Sheila to have another handy breakdown, but the contrary car was obviously on Dex's side. In typical fashion, she'd defied Beth and purred like a well-fed tiger.

As they'd finally cleared the city limits of Phoenix, Beth had walked her fingers slowly upward from Dex's knee until he'd finally been forced to either find a convenient deserted road or wrap Sheila around a fence post. Then, of course, Beth had needed an early lunch to refuel after their gymnastics.

Now, dressed and sprawled barefoot on the hood, she'd run out of delays. She settled back against his chest, nestled between his legs, and gazed blindly at the ecru and ocher of her nearly barren surroundings. Craggy rock formations thrust up from the desert floor, covered with tiny pockets of greenery, evidence of the season. Small rustlings and glimpses of shadow suggested that they were not entirely alone, but she didn't care about the small-animal population. Her thoughts were on her irrational desire to make time stop.

Dex finished a pear and tossed the core to the unseen creatures of the desert. He wrapped his arms around her, and she hesitantly cuddled into them. Her throat was tight and moisture blurred her vision. Maybe she should just take her wallet from its hiding place and go on alone. Wouldn't it be easier to make a clean, quick break than to torture herself with another day?

Then she shook her head, impatient with her maudlin—and impractical—mood. "Ready to go?" she asked briskly, making no move to pull away. "We have eleven hundred miles to cover."

"In a minute." His embrace tightened. "First you're going to tell me what all this is about."

She should have known he'd miss nothing, but she pressed on regardless. "All what?"

"All this." He kissed the top of her head. "You're stalling, and I want to know why."

Staring at a stray cloud scudding overhead, she commented, "There's the rain I predicted. You know, I never realized that desert showers were made up of single clouds dumping as they wander. I mean the whole sky doesn't—"

"Beth," he repeated patiently, "why are you stalling?"

Giving up on her diversion, she infused as much innocence into her tone as she could muster. "What makes you think I am?"

"Well," he mused, "I could chalk up most of the morning to your obsession with detail, but this last escapade was a dead giveaway." She could hear his smile. "As much as I enjoyed the novel experience of making love over a stick shift, I prefer a bed." He pondered it. "Or at least a carpet."

"Oh, dear. Don't tell me I forgot to warn you about my kinky tendencies." She clicked her tongue, blinking back her tears. "I guess now's not the time to describe the rowboat fantasy I've had since I was sixteen, huh?"

His voiced dropped to a husky murmur in her ear. "We'll wait until we're back on the Bay for that one."

She stiffened, her hand creeping automatically to her burning stomach. There it was, her nebulous fear put into words. He spoke of an indeterminate future with a certainty she was far from feeling. She loved him now, but couldn't he see that their return to reality would be a death knell? She'd reestablish her banking job, fighting the sharks as she always had, eventually forgetting "Beth" beneath the Velvet Hammer's ruthless force. Dex would continue his periodic self-employment, working when he felt like it, letting the days blend together with no goal in sight, and the Spiderman would eventually find the demure mate he needed—one who wouldn't suddenly devour him when he turned his back.

"Hey," he said, sensing her apprehension. Gently, he swung her around, peering at her with a puzzled frown. "What's this?" He brushed a droplet from her eye and kissed her tenderly. "Don't worry, honey," he whispered. "She'll be there."

That wasn't the problem, but she smiled anyway. Better to let him think her concern was totally about Jane. "What if she's not?" Amazingly, it honestly didn't concern her. Dex seemed convinced they'd find her, and she realized she trusted his quirky instincts. But she couldn't tell him that. "What if I scared her off?"

"Her ex-husband couldn't possibly recognize your voice, and with your usual brilliant caution, you didn't identify yourself or ask for Jane." He caressed her cheek. "C'mon, what happened to that reluctant optimism?"

"I think it locked itself in the toilet."

He chuckled. "Then let it out."

Her lip trembled and her gaze flickered over his face, memorizing every rugged feature. "As simple as that, huh?"

A tiny frown creased his brow. "Sure. Everything's as simple as you choose to make it, Beth."

Her heart pummeled her chest in an almost painful display of an emotion she couldn't, or wouldn't, identify. Dexter Wolffe, the most complicated man she'd ever known, always managed to make complex things sound so easy. And in twenty-four hours he would be gone.

Impulsively, she flung her arms around his neck, holding him as if she'd never let him go. She released him with the same suddenness, forcing a smile to her lips. "Okay, it's out." She slipped to the ground and shoved her feet into the flip-flops. "In fact," she went on with the same false brightness, "I'm going to study those dummy corporations while we drive. No harm in continuing our double-pincer strategy, right?" She leaped into Sheila and grabbed the printouts. "I can't shake the feeling that Mr. Bernard Schwartz is more than just the CEO of that Boston-based rope company." She glanced up to find Dex staring at her, obviously baffled by her abrupt change of mood. "Well?" she demanded. "Let's hit the road!"

He blinked, then shook his head sharply. After sliding off the hood, he opened his door and eased into his seat. As he started the engine, he frowned at her, then lowered his gaze and shook his head again. "You confuse the hell out of me, lady."

She grinned, the first real grin she'd mustered. "Good. Keeps you on your toes."

"If I'd wanted that," he said as he shifted into gear, "I'd have become a ballet dancer."

She appraised him, her pulse skittering at the memory of his body imprinted on hers but she squashed the fleeting emotion that brought. She would not ruin the rest of the trip by weeping all over his manly frame like a mourner in a bad Greek tragedy. "Too bad," she told him with a twinkle. "I really have a thing for men in tights."

His mouth twitched with a suppressed smile. "Boats and tights," he mused. "I'd better keep you on a leash when we get back to San Francisco."

She giggled for his benefit, then buried her nose in the papers to shut out his teasing intentions. How could she listen to them when her soul already ached so much, she could barely breathe? How could she talk when she'd already begun her farewell speech?

How could she plan a tomorrow when she'd begun to say her good-byes today?

Lost in their own thoughts, neither Dex nor Beth noticed the black Sundance with a dented rear bumper ease off the shoulder behind them.

By the time they'd left Tucson behind, the words on the printout had begun a strange pirouette on the paper. Beth rubbed her temples, forcing herself to focus. "Boston Twine and Cord," she muttered for the eightieth time. "Bernard Schwartz. Hmmm . . . nothing. Giant Oil, Inc., president Roy Fitzgerald—"

"'Fitz' means 'illegitimate son of.' Could that be significant?"

"Interesting, but I doubt it. He's the only Fitz." She squinted. "Allen Tobacco Company, Limited, paired with Nathan Birnbaum. Daydream Publishing—David Kaminsky. Marion Michael Morrison, Seabee Scrap and Metal. Shoot, that one looks familiar too. Leonard Slye, Evans Guitars. Li—" She straightened and ran her finger down the column. "Hey, I just realized! There are no women on this list, Dex."

"Oh, good. The bad guy's a woman-hater. That narrows it down to your entire executive board."

"True." She slumped in her seat, knuckled her eyes, and grabbed a boxed fruit juice from their stash of food. "Want one?"

He nodded. "Could there be a pattern in the letters, or initials?"

She glanced through and shook her head. "Not that I can see. Dammit, none of them are smart enough to concoct anything that elaborate. It has to be something so obvious, I'm not seeing it."

As she resolutely went back to her study, he reached over and slid the printouts from her lap. "Time for a break."

She snatched at them halfheartedly. "What are you doing?"

"Mandatory retirement," he told her firmly, slipping the printouts between his seat and the door. "You'll never find the answer by beating it into the ground. Relax."

"How?" she asked warily.

"By doing what you do best. Diverting attention."

She was good at that, she admitted ruefully, but

only for other people. For herself, she couldn't release a dilemma once she'd begun working on it. That workaholic syndrome he mistakenly thought a problem was usually a boon.

Then again, she realized, she'd had some whopping headaches in her life, and there was her blasted nervous stomach. Maybe he had a point, as he usually did. Fat chance of her admitting it, though.

He switched on the stereo and loaded a cassette. "Shut your eyes," he commanded, his voice lowering to a purr while the blank portion of the tape hissed over the speakers.

She obeyed with a sigh, crossing her arms. "Okay, give it your best shot."

He drew her locked elbows apart. "Tight posture, closed mind. Relax, Beth."

She resisted until the first, unmistakable strains of music surrounded her. Startled, her eyes flew open. "That's the theme song from *Gone with the Wind*!" She glanced at him. "When did you get this?"

"I found it at the thrift shop. It's full of old movie themes." His gaze warmed. "I can compromise, when the cause is worthy."

She disregarded his possible meaning, narrowing her eyes. "Any other little surprises?"

"What's the matter? Afraid of what else I sneaked past you?"

"You could have bought a regiment of elephants that day, and I would never have noticed," she muttered ruefully.

"I know," he said, his expression smug.

She opened her mouth for a sharp retort but found herself grinning instead. With a sigh, she settled into Sheila's upholstery and sipped her juice. She heard the ticking clock in her brain, but for once she refused to listen. Hadn't she decided it was counterproductive to dwell on things she couldn't change? Reality would catch up with them soon enough. When the time came, she would end it quickly and painlessly, as she knew was best for them both.

For now she would enjoy the present.

They passed the Arizona–New Mexico border as the cassette was beginning its third round. Dex replaced it with the Electric Light Orchestra and proceeded to find other diversions. He didn't have to work very hard; Beth was easy to agitate. And he had to admit her viewpoint fascinated him, challenging him on a level he'd neglected for a long, long time.

They discussed everything from movies to politics to soft drinks, but they agreed on very little. After splurging on triple-decker ice cream cones in Deming, he found yet another sensitive spot in the woman he loved. He admitted privately that it wasn't too difficult. Playing devil's advocate had always appealed to him, and this idealistic firebrand fascinated him. He'd never known anyone so unique.

And he realized their antagonism had always been suppressed hunger. Now that the prejudice and frustration were gone, it had simply taken on a new dimension.

"I'm telling you, space exploration is the only way to go!" she cried with conviction.

"That's your answer to the environmental problems? A disposable Earth?" He finished off his Butter Brickle in one massive gulp.

Her blue eyes flashed. "Of course not."

He glanced over and choked on his next word. Beth was licking the ice cream in long, slow sweeps, swirling it to a head, only to nibble it down. He clenched the steering wheel in a white-knuckled grip. His brain became toast even as his body saluted her ingenuity.

On the far side of El Paso, after bolstering his self-control with a reminder that the sooner they finished the sooner they could start their life together, Dex halted at a truck stop to buy gasoline. Though they'd filled the tank when they stopped for ice cream, he wanted to top it off. "If I remember correctly, there's nothing but farm roads, tumbleweeds, and oil wells until Van Horn," he told her. Then, at her questioning look, he said, "I did a job here a couple of years ago. I couldn't resist exploring a little."

The automatic shutoff clicked at the prepaid amount, and he bent to double-check the amount on the gauge, rolling his stiff neck as he did. A flash of sunlight caught his eye, but when he looked he saw only the tail end of a black compact disappearing around the corner of the cafe toward, if he remembered correctly, another set of pumps. He frowned. Why did that car niggle at his memory?

"Are there lots of motels?" she asked, her tone husky.

He dismissed the vague recollection as he focused on more important things. "Sorry, other than Van Horn and Fort Stockton, it's pretty barren until San Antonio, and that's five or six hundred miles away. We might as well push all the way through."

"Oh." Disappointed, she leaned her elbows on Sheila's hood, fanning herself as she stretched cramped muscles. He watched her, arousal surging forth again at the seductive glimpse of cleavage she showed, the tight length of leg beneath her jeans.

She eyed the stark, dry landscape past this oasis, an ocean of dirt that seemed to go on forever. "I can't believe that over two thirds of this trip will be across Texas. It's so *big*."

He forced his mind to the subject. "Didn't you ever live here?"

"Nope. It's one of the few places Dad neglected. I don't even know if there's a Marine base anywhere." She glanced at the angle of the relentless sun. "We're making good time, though. We should be in Van Horn by dusk, right?"

He nodded. "And Galveston by dawn." He frowned as he noticed Beth rubbing her stomach. "We're going to get that looked at in San Antonio."

"I'm fine," she said with a sigh. "It's hunger, that's all." A white panel truck roared up to the opposite pump as she muttered something else.

"What?"

"I'm getting sick of bologna!" she cried over the din. "And I hurt all over!"

Concerned, he walked behind her and began massaging with swift, sure strokes, glaring at the noisy contraption. As if responding, the engine ceased, its silence making Beth jump. The driver walked around, grabbed the nozzle, and spread his hands in mute apology. "Muffler's out," he explained, then tipped his hat at Beth. "Howdy, ma'am."

As the stocky man started feeding his monster, Dex felt her shoulders quiver. "Did he just say what I think he said?" she muttered under her breath. "And what was that on his hat?"

"The same logo's on the truck," he told her. "I think it's the name of a production company out of Dallas."

"Do you think they're shooting a movie around here?"

She couldn't hide her childlike excitement, and he grinned. "Possibly. But don't get your hopes up. We need to push on." She tensed beneath his fingers. "Beth," he warned, sensing her intentions. "No more delays."

"No!" She gasped. "Movies!"

"What about them?"

She began to bounce on her toes. "Dammit, concentrate," she muttered to herself. "Film, cameras, roll 'em, *something*."

He turned her, frowning at her tightly closed eyes and pinched mouth. Obviously, she was holding her breath. He briefly wondered if she was going to explode. "We don't have time to go find that movie set."

Her lids flew open; her breath whooshed out in one exasperated exhalation. "Give me a break, Dex. I swear sometimes I could strangle you. I—" She froze, her gaze unfocused. Then a radiant smile lit her face. "That's it!"

Giving a little squeal, she dove into Sheila, rummaging for the printouts. Baffled, he shook his head and leaned into the car, his neck twinging. She ran a finger down the list of dummy corporations.

"Bernard Schwartz," she murmured. "Boston Twine and Cord. Cute, real cute. And Seabee Scrap. Good grief, where has my brain been all this time?"

As she continued to mutter to herself, he tucked a stray strand of hair behind her ear and straightened. "Earth to Beth." She swiveled her head up, her mouth agape, as if she were surprised to find him there. He sighed. "Are you going to explain this or should I reserve you a rubber room somewhere?"

"Don't you see it?" She tapped the paper.

"Pretend I'm ignorant," he said dryly.

"I'm sorry," she said, chuckling. "I know I sound crazy, but—wait a minute. Let me show you." She crawled out and spread the sheets on Sheila's hood, pointing. "See? Bernard Schwartz." She shoved her curls from her cheeks and turned her shining face to him. "It was driving me nuts! I knew I'd heard that name, but I was thinking of *real people.*"

"And he's not a real person?"

"Yes, but—" She grinned. "It's not his real name." She grimaced. "I mean, it *is* his real name, but—"

"Beth."

She stomped her foot. "You're confusing me! Don't you see? It's the movies!"

He nodded, completely baffled. "No."

She closed her eyes and took a deep breath, enunciating clearly. "Bernard Schwartz is the legal name of Tony Curtis, 'The Boston Strangler.'"

Comprehension dawned, and his enthusiasm

grew. "You mean those are all the real names of movie stars?" He peered over her shoulder. "Marion Michael Morrison?"

"John Wayne, *The Fighting Seabees.* See? It's all here, tied to the names of the companies. David Kaminsky is Danny Kaye, who played two daydreamers—Walter Mitty and Hans Christian Andersen." Her voice began to fade, like an old Victrola that had wound down. "Roy Fitzgerald is Rock Hudson, I think, and Leonard Slye is— Leonard Slye is—" She broke off as if someone had slapped her, then went on. "Well, I'm not sure about him." She wiped perspiration from her pale brow. "But I'm pretty sure Nathan Birnbaum is George Burns. The cigar company, of course, and Gracie Allen was his wife." Her hand trembled.

"What's the matter?" he asked.

"Nothing, I—" A shudder rippled over her. "Damn," she whispered. "Reality check."

"Hey, it's okay." His arms crept around her waist. "Honey, it doesn't matter if you don't know them all." When she dropped her gaze, he brought it up, puzzled by her behavior. "You broke the case, partner."

"I did, didn't I?" Her tone suggested she'd accidentally shot herself in the foot.

"Yes, you did," he repeated. "Don't you get it? Only one of the suspects is that obsessed with old movies."

"No, Dex." She smiled sadly. "There are two. John Stein"—she shrugged—"and me."

She squeaked the last word, jabbing at his soul. "So?"

Tears welled in her eyes. "I just made everything worse, didn't I?"

"No, darlin'. All that means is the printouts don't prove anything by themselves."

She braced herself. "Which means you need to go back to trace the money to John."

He went cold. "Well, of course, but I wouldn't—"

Their gazes locked.

What he read stunned him. Excitement and pride and even a certain smug glint, yes. But beneath it all a sad kind of resignation darkened the depths. She opened her mouth to speak, then closed it, groping for words to suit her thoughts.

Good Lord, he thought, after all they'd been through together, could she still expect him to take her back to San Francisco?

This is all wrong!

Without pausing to analyze his actions, without finishing what he'd begun to tell her, he herded her into the car.

Startled, she went unresisting. "What are you doing?"

He slammed the door, refusing to answer as he hurried to the other side. He slid into the driver's seat, pausing when his fingers met the key. "If you want to leave," he said, his heart in his throat, "do it now. Otherwise"—he switched on the engine—"buckle up, partner."

She hesitated. "Where are we going?"

He held his breath. "You'll have to trust me on that."

Hand on the gearshift, he waited the longest minute of his life. He didn't know why she debated it so long, since she didn't have a penny to her name. He couldn't even fathom why he'd made the offer, since logic told him she had no real choice.

But, true to his word, he didn't shove it into first until he heard the click of the belt.

"I hate you," she muttered.

His heart started beating again; oxygen returned to his lungs. Dizzy, he gunned the engine. He didn't understand what had just happened, but she'd finally trusted him with her freedom, nothing but faith—and he hoped, despite her words, love—guiding her.

But as he glanced at her rigid, rebellious pose, he wondered if it was truly the step forward he'd thought, or had he inadvertently made his biggest mistake of all?

Five miles later he noticed the black Sundance, and, more important, he caught a glimpse of its driver. His pulse pounded in his ears, and when he heard a rhythmic click, he realized that he was tapping his ring against the steering wheel.

Nervous habits? he thought, remembering her amazement that he had none. He obviously had plenty that were just lying dormant, waiting for the perfect release.

And now was definitely the time. His instincts were obviously not infallible. His rational mind recoiled, but he realized he had no options left.

For the first time in his life, he had to plan.

Ten

Elizabeth sat huddled in the passenger seat, staring absently at her shadow as it danced over the dashboard. Picking at a thread in her jeans, she kicked herself mentally, fighting angry tears.

Idiot! she thought. By solving the riddle of those dummy corporations, she'd given him the ammunition to take charge again. Then, running true to form, she'd followed it up by blowing the perfect opportunity to leave. All she'd had to do was pull out her wallet, give him a brief "it was fun but never meant to be" speech, buy a bus ticket, and go on to Jane's alone. But no! She had to go all sentimental at the last minute and crawl meekly into the car!

She closed her eyes tightly and shivered. The Velvet Hammer had fallen harder than she'd thought.

"If you've finished your tantrum," Dex said mildly, "you might want to grab something solid. This isn't going to be smooth."

Startled, she glanced out the windshield to find not a highway but an exit ramp. Without a pause, he bounded onto a rutted dirt road that stretched to a low range of mountains.

Reflexively, she clutched her seat belt, snapping it tight at the first bump. Then she saw the pothole—or was it a miniature Grand Canyon?—directly in their path. And he was headed straight for it! "Slow down!" she cried. "What are you doing?"

Dex set his jaw and shifted gears, then floored the accelerator. He swerved around the gap, fish-tailing, spitting gravel. "I'm not sure you want to hear this, sweetheart," he muttered with a grim smile, "but we got ourselves a real live chase scene." He glanced in the rearview mirror. "And he's better than I thought."

"What?" Aghast, she swiveled her head around. Behind them, avoiding the crater with none of Dex's elegance but all of his speed, a black compact doggedly followed. The dust of their passage almost obscured it, but she had a sudden suspicion that its bumper was dented. "Dex," she whispered, "I think I saw that car in Phoenix."

"Really," he mused. "That's interesting."

"Why is it—*yeow!*" She shrieked as the tires skidded into the dry grass lining the route. She nailed him with furious blue eyes. "I knew that computerized brain of yours was too good to be true. You've finally cracked!"

They bounded back, and the car shuddered over the washboardlike surface. "What makes you say that?" he asked with a suspicious quiver of amusement.

"Because it might be the bad guys! Dammit,

didn't you think about that?" Her own voice vibrated, too, but not from laughter. The damn road made her sound like she was yelling through a fan, giving the whole nightmare situation comical overtones. But she was in no mood for humor. She wanted to tear his liver out! "Dex, you should have stayed on the highway. Sheila could have blown his doors off."

"Ah, but speeding cars attract all sorts of undesirable elements, like police. No one will see us out here."

She released her grip long enough to slap her forehead, nearly toppling into the dash. "How silly of me not to understand! Of course—we're *much* better off in the middle of nowhere." She slanted him a dry look. "Remind me to thank you for your brilliant plan when they finally find our dead bodies in a gully *twelve years from now*!"

He chuckled. "C'mon, Hammer, where's your sense of adventure?"

"It bailed out a mile ago," she said. "Along with my kidneys and Sheila's transmission!"

"Don't worry, I'll protect you."

"Gee, that reassures me a whole lot!" In truth, her fear of their pursuer was minor. She was too terrorized by Dex's maniacal driving to let a little thing like a possible murder upset her. Besides, she refused to let the criminal kill Dex. She wanted that pleasure for herself.

Her sarcasm was wasted anyway, since he chose that moment to downshift and gun the engine, climbing a slope that made San Francisco look like Kansas. Flattened into her seat by gravity, she could only close her eyes, clench her armrest, and pray that he knew what he was doing.

They topped the ridge and were suddenly air-borne. Her entire life flashed before her eyes in Technicolor. But before she had time to do more than gasp, they touched down with all the grace of an albatross.

Her teeth clamped together, pinching her tongue. Then the bottom dropped out of her stomach as they swooped into a gully. She yelped and prepared to blast Dex, his debatable piloting skills, and anything else that came to mind.

But she couldn't. Since her brain was oatmeal and her body a cold lump of clay, that didn't surprise her. What did, though, was the realization that beneath her terror, she was having *fun*!

As she worked to focus on her thoughts, Sheila slowed. With a flourish worthy of James Bond himself, Dex skidded to a halt at the bottom of the hill. He peered at the ridges surrounding them on four sides, then nodded. "This'll do," he said, and exited.

"We're on the ground?" she asked numbly. Her head spun as he opened her door. "Permission to throw up, Captain."

"Sorry, no time." He peeled her fingers off the dashboard and tugged. "Come on, sweetheart. He'll be here any second."

"He? Who, he?" She knew she sounded like a donkey, but she couldn't seem to get a grip on her thought processes.

He eased her to her feet. "You'll see."

She was vaguely aware that her knees wobbled like wet noodles, but she recognized the sensations now. Just after his return, her father had taken her on a corkscrewed roller coaster, to "build" her character. It had taken her a week to recover. The next day she'd begged him to return. "I think I need to sit down," she told Dex firmly, and plopped to the dirt.

"Very dignified, Ms. Hamner." He lifted her in his arms and set her on Sheila's hood. "Smile, sweetheart," he urged, and sat beside her, gazing up toward the ridge they'd just left.

"You smile," she spat out, but followed his line of vision. At the top, crouched like a vulture, the black Sundance waited, the afternoon sun glinting off its windshield. She held her breath, and her hand crept into Dex's. When she realized what she'd done, she tried to pull it back, but he squeezed it in a quick calming gesture.

After an eternal wait, the car began to creep down the hill, crunching over stones and bracken, picking up speed as it traveled. Beth's pulse quickened along with it, but she squinted through the reflected sunlight, attempting to at least discover who her opponent was.

When the car finally came to a stop before them, she identified the telltale dent in the rear, wiped a clammy palm over her jeans, and stared at the shadowy figure inside. It didn't take long for her eyes to click with her mind, with memories of a time that seemed so long ago, another life altogether. That grizzled gray head and broken nose could only belong to one person. "Dex," she said with a gasp. "It's Lieutenant Shaw!"

The squat police officer got out of the car and crunched toward them, shoving a stick of peppermint gum into his mouth as he walked.

Panic rushed in, freezing the blood in her veins. "He's going to arrest me!"

"He has no jurisdiction here," Dex murmured.

"Then what—" Startled, her gaze flew to Dex, his bland expression confirming her suspicions. "You knew it was him!"

It wasn't a question, but he nodded anyway. "I figured it was time for a showdown." He released their intertwined fingers. "And other things," he murmured cryptically.

For a moment she felt as if someone had kicked the supports from beneath her, but she tilted her chin up a notch and folded her arms over her chest, refusing to acknowledge the stab in her heart as she faced the policeman. "Fancy meeting you here, Lieutenant."

"Call me Harry," he said. "This, uh, isn't official business."

She suddenly realized he didn't look grim at all. In fact, as he shoved his hands into his pockets, she detected a distinctly sheepish smile. She frowned, confused. "What do you want, then?"

He shrugged. "I just happened to be in the neighborhood."

Dex snorted. "You can do better than that."

Suspicious, she pivoted from one man to the other. Her gaze narrowed on Dex. "What's going on?" she asked.

The mocking corner of his mouth lifted. "Harry's been following us for days," he explained. "Since Jane's house, to be exact. He saw us search the place, then trailed us and waited on the corner of that dead end."

"I must be slipping," Harry said. "But I should have guessed you'd spotted me when you made me wander Papago Park for hours. If I hadn't seen you racing out of the zoo, I would never have found you again. Do you know how many motels there are in Phoenix?"

"He searched our room too. Remember the gum wrapper you found?"

"But why?" Before either man could answer, she said, "You're not after me, you're after *Jane*!" At Shaw's nod, her head whirled. She closed her eyes tightly against the spinning scenery. "Do you know how much trouble you could have saved me if you'd *told* me you were going to go looking for my witness!"

"I didn't know myself until after the Feds took over. We honestly didn't have the manpower to spare; they were just too convinced you were guilty to bother." His expression hardened. "I don't like having a suspect railroaded because someone's too cocky to check all avenues."

Another thought occurred to her, and her relief disappeared, replaced with an icy knot in the pit of her stomach. Defying that irritating weakness, she turned to Dex. "How long have you known?" she asked, her tone low and dangerous.

"About a half an hour before we pulled off the highway. I'd caught glimpses of the car, but it's a common make. I couldn't pin down my apprehension." This time his smile mocked only himself. "I'm a great detective, huh?"

His prompt answer, steady gaze, and most of all, sarcastic humility convinced her. Dex had done a lot of things, but he had never lied to her.

But, dammit, that raised even more questions! Maybe her brain was still rattled from Mr. Wolffe's wild ride, but she could voice only one of them, and her throat tightened with the implications. "Then what are we doing here, Spiderman?"

Though part of her knew that he'd never let anyone harm her, the wary and far larger part smelled a setup. "Come on, you didn't drag us out to this—" she waved a hand at their stark surroundings, striving for a touch of her old acid— "this truly beautiful sylvan spot just so you could play Charlie Chan, did you?"

"I was kind of wondering about that myself," Harry said when Dex didn't reply.

"Actually," he said, sliding to the ground. "I decided it was time to roll the credits."

Elizabeth was vaguely aware of Harry's baffled "Huh?" but it made perfect sense to her. He was terminating their relationship early, the coward. "I see." Moisture pricked her eyelids. Why did she cry so much lately? Impatiently, she blinked it away and nodded. "It wasn't enough that you were going to take me back to San Francisco, you had to rub salt into the wound first."

Dex continued to hold her gaze. "Beth, for one of the smartest people I've ever known, you're pretty dense sometimes. You were so busy hating me that you didn't even notice I was going east, not west, on the highway."

"What? Then . . ." Her brow creased.

His gray eyes softened. "I promised you a double-pincer, Hammer. I wouldn't go back on my word. Now that we know John Stein is the embezzler, it won't take more than a day or so to track the stolen funds. With the testimony Jane's sure to have, you'd never have to go to jail."

Confused, but no less angry, she scowled at him. "But?"

He opened his mouth, closed it, and shrugged, leaning against Sheila's hood. "But when I saw

Harry, it suddenly occurred to me that no matter what I did, even if I'd explained it then, you'd blame me somehow. I never intended to abandon you, but in your mind I did the next best thing—I made the decision for you."

"Yes," she said steadily, "you did."

"I know." He dropped his gaze to his finger, to the sparkle of his dark ring in the sunlight. "I'm not noble enough to smile and tell you to go with Harry to Galveston. But contrary to your opinion of me, I'm also not selfish enough to drag you back to San Francisco while I trace that money to the source."

She clenched her icy hands together. "So you decided to give me a choice, instead."

His head snapped up at her frigid tone. "I don't want to box you in," he told her. "You needed alternatives."

Her body trembled as she leashed her temper, and her misery. "I didn't need you to give them to me," she said, only her voice quavering. "But as usual, you're calling the shots, aren't you?" She stepped back. "Thanks, *partner*. For nothing." She turned slowly, trusting her sense of direction alone for guidance, since she couldn't see a blasted thing. "Harry? Do you have room for one more?"

"Beth—"

She halted, stiffening. "What?"

"I blew it, didn't I? You're leaving anyway."

She swallowed hard. "Yes," she said hoarsely.

"One more thing you have to know. I love you."

For a moment her heart soared. She reeled as her yearning washed through her, letting her know how much she'd ached to hear those words from him.

Then, as she realized his intent, her fury rose like a tidal wave, overwhelming any trace of elation.

She whirled around, her hair flying every which way as she strode to him. "That was low," she said, "even for you. Don't you dare manipulate me like that. You have to be right, don't you? You have to know everything. Well, not this time, Spiderman. This time, you were wrong!"

"I just wanted to give you the true bittersweet ending you want."

She gritted her teeth against the sob that rose in her throat. "It's not up to you, dammit! It's up to me." She pointed to her chest. "Me, Dex, not you! Do you understand now? It's my decision!"

"I understand."

His voice broke. Dashing the tears from her eyes, she glared at him with all the anger and hurt she felt.

But as she prepared to let it loose, she recognized the agony behind his steady gray eyes, noted the rapid pulse beating in his temple, the sheen of perspiration on his brow.

This wasn't some game he was playing to bait and taunt her. He really loved her!

As she looked away, something inside her fell with a resounding crash, peeling away the layers of pain she'd never realized colored her views before now. He was right. She wanted to pin the blame on him to avoid the emotional confrontation she knew was to come. She'd been the manipulator, not him, maneuvering them closer to an ending she understood, that she could handle and control. She'd been prepared to walk away from him, keeping her dreams of what might have been close to her heart, where they were safe.

She preferred the bittersweet endings, because that's all life had shown her. She'd rebelled against the complicated net in which she'd found herself ensnared, yet she'd built it, not Dex, and she'd pulled it tighter with every day that had passed. Because it wasn't the prison she'd once thought. It was a sweet, golden web, liberating her real soul as it tangled reassuringly around her, protecting yet never hampering the strength she thought she'd lose if she gave in.

She'd lost nothing. She'd only gained. Subconsciously—no, instinctively—she'd always known.

And she had the proof.

Feeling raw and exposed, she slowly paced around Sheila and opened her door. Slipping her hand behind her seat, she pulled out her wallet, then walked over to Dex. Unable to meet his eyes, she stared at the lowest button on his shirt, a foggy blob of white, and held out her evidence on shaking hands. "I found this yesterday, before we raided the computer lab," she whispered.

She saw him stiffen. "You think I took it?"

"No," she told him honestly, vaguely surprised that it had never entered her mind. She was also faintly annoyed that he didn't get her point.

"I see." He slumped. "I guess this means you don't even need Harry. You could have—" He broke off with a gasp. "You could have gone on by yourself, anyway!"

Hope brightened his expression, filling her heart to overflowing. "And?" she prompted.

He cradled her cheeks in his palms. She felt him tremble. "And?" she repeated.

"And . . ." He searched her face, almost in disbelief. She saw the exact moment that it hit him. "And you had it last night, before we made love," he whispered.

"Bingo." The flood washed down her cheeks as she made the hardest admission of all. "I love you."

He lowered his mouth to hers, kissing her with a reverence she'd never perceived before now. But it had always been there. She'd just been too "focused" to notice.

Worship, however, was the furthest thing from her mind. With a moan, she deepened the kiss, delving into his warm mouth with the hunger she'd felt that very first time, the desire she'd stifled for years beneath her so-called competitive nature, the passion that was her true strength.

Harry cleared his throat with such force that even her lust-soaked mind realized it was the latest of many attempts to get their attention. She felt Dex smile as her watery giggle burst forth, and she lowered her forehead to his chest for a moment before glancing over at the red-faced policeman. "Harry, I have a favor to ask."

"You want a fire extinguisher?"

"No. I still need to get Jane back to San Francisco." For a single instant she saw a flash of suspicion in Dex's gray eyes, but she couldn't blame him. Her single-minded pursuit had ruined more than one romantic scene. But now that they had money again—and her love for Dex had destroyed her mistrustful barriers—she had a world of possibilities open before her.

Never breaking eye contact, reassuring him with every fiber of her being, she called to Harry. "Hank's Bait Shop. Galveston, Texas."

"What's that?"

She nuzzled Dex's nose with hers. "That's where Jane is holed up. Don't let her get away, Harry."

Dex smiled and caressed her stubborn chin. "I love you," he whispered. She kissed his thumb.

"Aren't you going after her?" Harry asked.

"No." She dropped the wallet to the ground. "We're going to El Paso."

"What's in El Paso?"

"Computers. I happen to know a certain brilliant programmer who worked there once, and I think he could pull a few strings to use their system to trace a dollar or two." She grinned as comprehension dawned on her beloved's face. "We have a few hunches to follow up on, Harry." Her arms twined around Dex's neck. "Don't we *partner*?" she whispered, only for him.

"A few," he murmured, brushing her lips with his. "And a lot of plans to make . . . partner."

As Harry drove away, before her eyes had quite fluttered closed, she noticed a spiky silhouette on the ridge behind Dex. She blinked, shook her head, and stared again. "Dex? I think we have an audience."

Frowning, he followed her line of vision. "Are those Indians?" he asked.

"The production company!" she said with a gasp, then turned her shining expression to his. "Think we have time to stop in and watch for a while?"

"I think we have all the time in the world," he told her, lowering his face to hers once more. His mouth halted right in front of hers. "Sweetheart? Isn't Leonard Slye the real name of Roy Rogers?"

"That's not important now."

"I agree."

"Will miracles never cease?"

"Shut up and kiss me."

"Roll credits on a happy ending," she said, then

joined her spirit with his in a true demonstration of the word.

Many hours later, the white charger called Sheila puffed into the sunset. Hand in hand, linked body and soul, the erstwhile Velvet Hammer and the mysterious man known as the Spiderman planned their new life together, one filled with peace, love, and harmony.

Sort of.

". . . and once we're married, of course, we'll—"

"Married? Hey, wait one minute, buster! Did it ever occur to you to *ask* me to marry you? I have a career, I have—"

"But, Beth, that job is unhealthy. A woman with a nervous stomach doesn't belong in corporate America!"

"Don't bully me, dammit. Take a look at yourself first! Why can't you take on that federal task force you told me about?"

"A suit? You want me to wear a suit? Are you nuts?"

"Well, if I ran for political office as you—ahem— *suggested*, what did you think you'd have to wear then? Husbands of candidates rarely run around in jeans and sweaters."

"Husband? Didn't it occur to you to wait for my proposal before you started making these broad assumptions?"

"Of course it did. But I decided to trust my instincts, instead."

"I think you made the right choice, love."

"Yeah. Me too."

THE EDITOR'S CORNER

Nothing could possibly put you in more of a carefree, summertime mood than the six LOVESWEPTs we have for you next month. Touching, tender, packed with emotion and wonderfully happy endings, our six upcoming romances are real treasures.

The first of these priceless stories is SARAH'S SIN by Tami Hoag, LOVESWEPT #480, a heart-grabbing tale that throbs with all the ecstasy and uncertainty of forbidden love. When hero Dr. Matt Thorne is injured, he finds himself recuperating in his sister's country inn—with a beautiful, untouched Amish woman as his nurse. Sarah Troyer's innocence and sweetness make the world seem suddenly new for this world-weary Romeo, and he woos her with his masterful bedside manner. The brash ladies' man with the bad-boy grin is Sarah's romantic fantasy come true, but there's a high price to pay for giving herself to one outside the Amish world. You'll cry and cheer for these two memorable characters as they risk everything for love. A marvelous LOVESWEPT from a very gifted author.

From our very own Iris Johansen comes a LOVESWEPT that will drive you wild with excitement—A TOUGH MAN TO TAME, #481. Hero Louis Benoit is a tiger of the financial world, and Mariana Sandell knows the danger of breaching the privacy of his lair to appear before him. Fate has sent her from Sedikhan, the glorious setting of many of Iris's previous books, to seek out Louis and make him a proposition. He's tempted, but more by the mysterious lady herself than her business offer. The secret terror in her eyes arouses his tender, protective instincts, and he vows to move heaven and earth to fend off danger . . . and keep her by his side. This grand love story will leave you breathless. Another keeper from Iris Johansen.

IN THE STILL OF THE NIGHT by Terry Lawrence, LOVESWEPT #482, proves beyond a doubt that nothing could be more romantic than a sultry southern evening. Attorney Brad Lavalier certainly finds it so, especially when he's stealing a hundred steamy kisses from Carolina Palmette. A heartbreaking scandal drove this proud beauty from her Louisiana hometown years before, and now she's back to settle her grandmother's affairs. Though she's stopped believing in the magic of love, working with devilishly sexy Brad awakens a long-denied hunger within her. And only he can slay the dragons of her past and melt her resistance to a searing attraction. Sizzling passion and deep emotion—an unbeatable combination for a marvelous read from Terry Lawrence.

Summer heat is warming you now, but your temperature will rise even higher with ever-popular Fayrene Preston's newest LOVESWEPT, FIRE WITHIN FIRE, #483. Meet powerful businessman Damien Averone, brooding, enigmatic—and burning with need for Ginnie Summers. This alluring woman bewitched him from the moment he saw her on the beach at sunrise, then stoked the flame of his desire with the entrancing music of her guitar on moonlit nights. Only sensual surrender will soothe his fiery ache for the elusive siren. But Ginnie knows the expectations that come with deep attachment, and Damien's demanding intensity is overwhelming. Together these tempestuous lovers create an inferno of passion that will sweep you away. Make sure you have a cool drink handy when you read this one because it is hot, hot, hot!

Please give a big and rousing welcome to brand-new author Cindy Gerard and her first LOVESWEPT—MAVERICK, #484, an explosive novel that will give you a charge. Hero Jesse Kincannon is one dynamite package of rugged masculinity, sex appeal, and renegade ways you can't resist. When he returns to the Flying K Ranch and fixes his smoldering gaze on Amanda Carter, he makes her his own, just as he did years before when she'd been the foreman's young daughter and he was the boss's son. Amanda owns half the ranch now, and Jesse's sudden reappearance is suspicious. However, his outlaw kisses soon convince her that he's after her heart. A riveting romance from one of our New Faces of '91! Don't miss this fabulous new author!

Guaranteed to brighten your day is SHARING SUNRISE by Judy Gill, LOVESWEPT #485. This utterly delightful story features a heroine who's determined to settle down with the only man she has ever wanted . . . except the dashing, virile object of her affection doesn't believe her love has staying power. Marian Crane can't deny that as a youth she was filled with wanderlust, but Rolph McKenzie must realize that now she's ready to commit herself for keeps. This handsome hunk is wary, but he gives her a job as his assistant at the marina—and soon discovers the delicious thrill of her womanly charms. Dare he believe that her eyes glitter not with excitement over faraway places but with promise of forever? You'll relish this delectable treat from Judy Gill.

And be sure to look for our FANFARE novels next month— three thrilling historicals with vastly different settings and times. Ask your bookseller for A LASTING FIRE by the bestselling author of THE MORGAN WOMEN, Beverly Byrne, IN THE SHADOW OF THE MOUNTAIN by the beloved Rosanne Bittner, and THE BONNIE BLUE by LOVESWEPT's own Joan Elliott Pickart.

Happy reading!

With every good wish,

Carolyn Nichols

Carolyn Nichols
Publisher, FANFARE and LOVESWEPT

60 Minutes to a Better, More Beautiful You!

Now it's easier than ever to awaken your sensuality, stay slim forever—even make yourself irresistible. With Bantam's bestselling subliminal audio tapes, you're only 60 minutes away from a better, more beautiful you!

__ 45004-2	**Slim Forever**	$8.95
__ 45035-2	**Stop Smoking Forever**	$8.95
__ 45022-0	**Positively Change Your Life** ...	$8.95
__ 45041-7	**Stress Free Forever**	$8.95
__ 45106-5	**Get a Good Night's Sleep**	$7.95
__ 45094-8	**Improve Your Concentration** .	$7.95
__ 45172-3	**Develop A Perfect Memory**	$8.95

Bantam Books, Dept. LT, 414 East Golf Road, Des Plaines, IL 60016

Please send me the items I have checked above. I am enclosing $_____ (please add $2.50 to cover postage and handling). Send check or money order, no cash or C.O.D.s please. (Tape offer good in USA only.)

Mr/Ms _____

Address _____

City/State _____ Zip _____

LT-2/91

Please allow four to six weeks for delivery.
Prices and availability subject to change without notice.

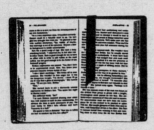